Felony at the Fall Festival
A Molly Montgomery Cozy Mystery

Tessa Aura

Contents

Chapter 1

PREPARATIONS

"H ey!" I swatted Jake's arm, laughing as he smirked down at me. "If you're not going to help, at least don't slow me down."

Jake's grin widened and his hazel eyes gleamed with mischief. "I'm helping, alright. Just keeping you from working too hard. Wouldn't want you pulling a muscle before the festival even starts."

I rolled my eyes, adjusting the banner we were hanging over the entrance to Maplewood Haven, the bed and breakfast I inherited from my aunt. The fall festival was just days away, and the whole town was buzzing with excitement. The Haven was filled with guests, and every corner of town seemed to be in full preparation mode. This place needed to be just as perfect as the rest of Maple Lake, and while Jake seemed more focused on teasing me, I was determined to get things done.

"Uh-huh, because clearly I'm the one slacking off," I shot back, grabbing the other end of the banner and stepping onto the small ladder.

Jake stood behind me, pretending to steady the ladder, but I knew he was looking for another excuse to mess with me. "You know, you could just let me do all the heavy lifting. You're the brains of this operation, anyway."

"Right," I snorted. "And the muscles are all yours, huh?"

"Exactly," he flexed his arm dramatically. "I'm the brawn, babe. You're the beauty."

"Beauty *and* brains," I corrected, tying the last knot. I hopped down from the ladder and dusted off my hands. "Now, if you're done flexing, can we please get back to work?"

Jake stepped closer, looping an arm around my waist and pulling me against him. "You're always so serious. Why don't you let me take you out for lunch? We can leave the decorations for a little bit, sneak off to The Maple Mug for some of Clara's famous cider—"

I wriggled free, laughing. "Jake, you are impossible."

He winked. "You love it."

And, annoyingly, I did. But there was no time for flirting when there was still so much to do. The fall festival wasn't just any old celebration in Maple Lake—it was the event of the year. People came from all around to partake in the pumpkin contest, the pie bake-off, and the warm, comforting drinks brewed at Clara's café. I wanted everything to go off without a hitch, especially with the influx of guests staying at Maplewood Haven.

"Alright, fine," Jake relented, reaching for the stack of hay bales by the entrance. "You've twisted my arm. I'll help."

"You should be thanking me," I said, grabbing a few corn stalks to arrange by the front door. "If we don't get this place looking festive, we'll have Edith Patterson on our case. You know how she gets during festival time. She takes her role as coordinator way too seriously."

Jake groaned in mock horror. "Don't remind me. Last year, she cornered me at the general store and lectured me about my 'lackluster pumpkin carving skills.'"

I burst out laughing. "She's a bit of a menace, but you've got to admit, the festival always turns out well."

"A *bit* of a menace?" Jake muttered, perfectly stacking the hay bales next to the porch.

I smiled as he wandered off. The inn was coming together nicely. Maplewood Haven always looked its best during the fall festival with garlands of autumn leaves, pumpkins lining the front porch, and candles flickering in every corner. The scent of baking pies and hot cider brewing in the kitchen made it feel even cozier.

Lila had popped in earlier to say hello before heading over to Max's pet store. I could already picture her leaning over the counter, all smiles and soft giggles, while Max pretended not to notice the way she flirted. It had been a slow burn between the two of them, but it was obvious to anyone watching—they were falling for each other.

As if on cue, my phone buzzed with a message from Lila: At Max's. He's pretending to be busy, but I'm wearing him down.

I chuckled to myself, imagining the scene. Max was meticulous with his store, especially after a recent incident he'd found himself in involving illegal snake trading. He was back on his feet, more focused than ever and running his shop with an emphasis on "normal pets"—dogs, cats, birds, and the occasional hamster or guinea pig. The illegal exotics were long gone, but Max's passion for animals remained.

I quickly texted back: Let him do his thing. You'll be able to charm him later.

She responded with a winking emoji, and I shook my head, smiling as I pocketed the phone.

I wasn't the only one excited for the fall festival—everyone in town had been buzzing about it for weeks. It was the biggest event of the year with food stalls, craft booths, and of course, the pumpkin contest. People took their pumpkins seriously around here. Last year's winner,

Mr. Thompson, had raised a gourd so big it took three men to lift it onto the stage. He was already talking about how he'd top that this year, and I could practically hear the groans from Jake, who always got roped into helping.

And then there was the festival's main attraction: Maplewood Haven's bake-off, hosted on the front lawn of the inn. The locals would compete for the title of best pie, cake, or bread, and the judges were always a mix of long-time residents and visitors. It was meant to be a good-natured competition, but there were always a few rivals who took it more seriously than others.

I glanced out the window, watching the townspeople setting up stalls and stringing lights across Main Street.

Jake came back into the room, carrying a box of candles this time. "What's next, boss?" he teased.

I looked around, noting the garlands, pumpkins, and flickering candles that were slowly filling the room. The cozy warmth of it all made me feel content like everything was falling into place. "I think we're just about done here. I'll finish up the kitchen, and then maybe you can help me with the outdoor lights?"

Jake nodded, setting the box down. "Sounds good. But first, I'm going to grab another piece of that pumpkin bread."

I laughed, waving him off as he headed back into the kitchen. The truth was, moments like this—working side by side with Jake, getting ready for something as simple as the fall festival—made me feel more at home than I had in a long time. Maplewood Haven had always been special, but now, with Jake by my side, it felt like home in a way I hadn't expected.

As I started tidying up, the door to the inn swung open, and Lila breezed in, her cheeks flushed from the cool autumn air. "You will not believe the day I've had," she said, dropping her bag on the nearest chair and plopping down beside it.

I raised an eyebrow, smirking. "Oh, let me guess—you spent the last two hours flirting with Max and pretending to care about chinchillas?"

She gave me a mischievous grin. "He's so easy to mess with. I swear, I asked him how to take care of a hamster, and the poor guy nearly knocked over a display of bird cages trying to find me a brochure."

I laughed, wiping my hands on my apron. "You're terrible. You know that, right?"

Lila waved me off, her eyes twinkling. "Please, he loves it. Anyway, I think I'm finally making progress. He asked me to help him pick out decorations for his window display tomorrow."

"Uh-huh, sounds like work," I teased. "Real romantic."

She laughed, settling into the chair with a contented sigh. "I don't need romance. I just need him to keep fumbling around with pet supplies while I look cute."

We both laughed, the sound filling the warm, cozy space of the inn. It felt good, this rhythm we'd found—preparing for the festival, teasing each other, flirting with the guys we liked. There was something so satisfying about it, like the pieces of our lives were finally falling into place.

Chapter 2

THE BODY

The fall festival had been in full swing all day. The Mayor, Vincent Harrison, had kicked it all off with his long boastful speech as usual. He was all decked out in his three-piece suit, bow tie, and showy pocket watch. He topped off the ensemble with a pair of white gloves. I was surprised he wasn't wearing his top hat.

It had been a long chaotic first day of festivities, but now the streets of Maple Lake were quiet. The stalls, booths, and tents had been closed for the day. Most of the townsfolk had turned in for the night, their bellies full of pie and cider, and their laughter lingering in the cool night air. The warm glow of string lights still twinkled above the square, casting long shadows over the festival tents.

Jake and I arrived back at the inn with Mitz, my chihuahua, in tow. I was about to unlock the front door when, out of nowhere, Mitz started yapping incessantly. I placed my hand on his head, rubbing softly to calm him down. He scoffed as if telling me to take my hands off. Although he quieted down, his ears remained perked. "Did you hear that?" I asked, turning toward a faint sound that drifted on the cool evening breeze. It was a strange noise—a rustling and a thud, followed by what sounded like the distant echo of a shout.

Mitz let out a low growl, his head snapping in the direction of the strange noise.

"What is it, boy?" Jake replied, but his brow furrowed as he glanced toward town and the dimly lit festival grounds. "It's not like Mitz to act like this."

I shivered, pulling my coat tighter around me. "Maybe it's just the wind," I said, trying to shake off the apprehension that was creeping in. But there was something about the stillness of the night that didn't sit right with me. Mitz yapped again.

Jake reached out, gently tugging me closer. "Come on, let's head inside. It's been a long day."

I nodded, my mind already starting to settle as we turned back toward the door. But just as I was about to push it open, there it was again—a sound, clearer this time. A thud. A heavy, unmistakable thud.

Jake stopped in his tracks. "Stay here," he said, his voice low and serious.

"Jake—" I started, but he was already moving toward the sound. His strides were purposeful and determined. I hesitated for a moment, torn between staying put like he'd asked and the gnawing feeling that something was terribly wrong.

I considered putting Mitz inside, but he was determined to come along. We followed Jake through the rows of tents, their canvas flaps rustling in the night breeze. The sweet scent of leftover caramel apples and roasted nuts hung in the air, but beneath it, there was something else. Something metallic. I wrinkled my nose; the smell made my stomach turn as we neared the back of the festival grounds.

Jake stopped suddenly, his hand going up to signal for me to stay back. But I was already beside him, my breath catching in my throat as I saw what he was looking at.

A body.

Lying in the shadows, crumpled behind one of the tents, was the figure of a man. His clothes were dirty, his face pale under the flickering glow of the string lights above. His chest was still, unmoving.

"Oh, my...," I whispered, my hand flying to my mouth. "Look, Jake." I pointed at a pocketknife covered in blood, laying only a couple of feet from the victim.

Jake knelt beside the man, carefully searching for a pulse. He shook his head. "He's gone."

For a moment, neither of us said anything. The quiet of the night seemed to press down on us, thick and suffocating. My mind raced, trying to make sense of what we were seeing. I didn't recognize the man—he wasn't from Maple Lake. His clothes were rumpled, and there was something about him that looked... out of place.

"What do we do?" I asked, my voice barely above a whisper.

Jake stood, his face set in a grim expression. "We need to call the police."

I fumbled for my phone, and my fingers trembled as I dialed the number. While I waited for the call to connect, my eyes drifted back to the body. Who was he? And what was he doing here?

***

By the time the police arrived, word had already started to spread. In a small town like Maple Lake, it didn't take long for news to travel. The sight of flashing lights and the presence of officers combing through the festival grounds drew a crowd, even at this late hour.

Mrs. Jenkins was one of the first to arrive, her coat hastily thrown over her nightgown as she hobbled over, clutching her cane with one hand and a mug of tea with the other.

"Did you hear, Molly?" she called out, her voice filled with the kind of morbid curiosity that only Mrs. Jenkins could muster. "A body! Right here in our little town. Haven't seen something like this since... well, a while!"

I forced a tight smile, my insides still churning from the sight of the stranger lying in the shadows. "Yeah, Mrs. Jenkins. It's terrible."

"I heard he's not from around here," she continued, sidling up beside me, her sharp eyes scanning the scene as the officers worked. "A drifter, maybe. Or worse."

I didn't have the energy to entertain her gossip, so I just nodded. My eyes darted toward Jake, who was talking to one of the officers near the tents.

The crowd grew as more people trickled in. All of them whispering, exchanging glances, wondering who the man was and what had happened. It didn't take long for the rumors to start.

"I bet it was someone passing through. Someone who got into trouble with the wrong crowd," Clara said, her voice low but urgent as she leaned in to talk to someone. I couldn't really make out faces right now. I was still shocked.

"Or maybe he was here for the festival," Betsy replied thoughtfully, her hands on her hips as she watched the officers. "Could've been someone looking to cause trouble."

Maggie shook her head, her brow furrowed. "I don't like it. It's not like Maple Lake to have something like this happen. And right in the middle of the festival, too."

I listened to their chatter, my mind still trying to piece together the night's events. Whoever the man was, he didn't seem like someone who had just wandered into town for the festival. There was something deliberate about the way he had been found—hidden as if someone had wanted to keep him out of sight.

The police were thorough, asking questions, taking statements, and making sure the area was secured. But even as they worked, there was an undercurrent of apprehension that settled over the crowd. This was Maple Lake—a cozy, tight-knit town where things like this didn't happen.

Jake eventually made his way back to me, his face serious. "The officers are looking into it, but there's no ID on the guy. They're not sure who he is yet."

I nodded, the heaviness of the last hour's events pressing down on my shoulders. "Do they have any idea what happened?"

"Not yet. But they'll figure it out." His hand found mine, giving it a reassuring squeeze. "Come on, let's get you inside. It's been a long night."

As we made our way back to the inn, the crowd still buzzing behind us, I couldn't shake the feeling that this was only the beginning. Whoever that man was, his presence in Maple Lake was going to stir things up. And I had a sinking feeling that the peaceful little town we all loved was about to change.

***

The next morning, the town was alive with gossip. As soon as I stepped into The Maple Mug for my usual morning coffee, I was greeted by a chorus of voices speculating about the dead man.

"I heard he was some kind of criminal," Mrs. Jenkins said, her voice carrying over the hum of conversation. "Probably on the run from the law."

"Oh, please," Clara interjected from behind the counter, pouring coffee with one hand and waving Mrs. Jenkins off with the other. "You don't know that."

I slid into my usual seat at the counter, feeling the eyes of the café's patrons on me as I did. "Morning, Clara," I said, offering her a tired smile.

"Morning, Molly," she replied, her face softening as she placed a steaming mug of coffee in front of me. "Rough night?"

"You could say that." I wrapped my hands around the warm cup, hoping it would calm my frayed nerves.

Clara leaned in, lowering her voice. "How are you holding up? I heard you and Jake were the ones who found him."

I nodded, taking a sip of coffee. "Yeah, we did. It was... unexpected, to say the least."

Clara shook her head, glancing around the café. "This whole town's going to be talking about it for weeks."

She wasn't wrong. As the morning wore on, more and more people filtered in, all of them eager to share their theories about who the man was and what had happened to him. By the time I left the café, my head was spinning with all the speculation.

***

As I stepped out of The Maple Mug, the morning light did little to dispel the shadows of the previous night. I was still processing the grim discovery Jake and I had made. The weight of the situation seemed to follow me as I walked back to Maplewood Haven.

The festival grounds, now empty and eerily quiet, were a stark contrast to the lively atmosphere of the day before. The tents and booths stood as silent witnesses to the night's events, their colorful decorations now appearing out of place against the backdrop of the ongoing investigation.

I made my way to the inn, where Jake was already waiting. He had promised to meet me after a quick check-in with the police. As soon as I entered, I could see the concern etched on his face.

"Are you ok?" he asked, his eyes searching mine for any sign of distress.

I nodded, though the tightness lingered in my chest. "I think so. Just trying to wrap my head around everything."

Jake pulled me into a hug, his warmth a small comfort against the chill that had settled over me. "We'll get through this. The police are on it, and we'll help however we can."

The sound of the doorbell interrupted our moment, and I glanced over to see Lila walking in, her expression one of worry and determination. She must have heard the news and wanted to check on us.

"Hey, Lila," I said, forcing a smile as I wiped away a stray tear.

Lila stepped inside, shaking her head as she took off her coat. "I wanted to make sure you two are alright. I heard about the body last night and thought I'd check in."

"We're ok, just shaken," Jake said. "It's been a rough start to the festival."

Lila nodded, her gaze shifting to the festival grounds visible through the inn's large windows. "I can't believe this happened. Maple Lake has always been so peaceful."

"I know," I agreed, my thoughts drifting back to the scene behind the tent. "And it's not just about the shock. There's something about the way he was found—tucked behind that tent like that. It feels deliberate."

Lila's brow furrowed as she considered this. "Do you think he was targeted?"

"It's hard to say," Jake said. "But the way he was positioned, it makes me think there was some intent behind it."

Just then, we heard the familiar chime of the doorbell once again. It was Betsy Hollis, the town historian. Beside her stood Ethel Potts, the owner of Main Street Bakery, holding a basket of baked goods. Their faces wore a mix of curiosity and concern.

"Oh, sweet Molly!" Mrs. Potts said gently. "I thought you might need a little pick-me-up." She glanced into the sitting room where a few guests had joined Jake and Lila. "I brought enough for everyone."

"Thanks, Mrs. Potts," I said, appreciating the warmth of her gesture. "That's really thoughtful."

I led the ladies to the sitting area and passed around the basket of pastries before choosing a warm apple spice muffin for myself. By the time I took my first bite, the conversation had already turned to the tragedy.

"He was just at my booth yesterday, asking about the town's history," Betsy exclaimed in disbelief. "Something about old records and local secrets."

"That's interesting," Lila's eyes narrowed as she considered this new detail. "Do you think he might have stumbled onto something he wasn't supposed to?"

Betsy leaned in, her expression troubled. "Maybe. It's clear he wasn't just a random visitor. There's something more to this."

I took a deep breath, trying to calm my racing thoughts. "It's hard to believe someone in Maple Lake would do something like this, but the way he was tucked away... It does make you wonder."

Lila sipped her coffee, her eyes thoughtful. "What if someone wanted to keep him from finding out too much? Or maybe he was on the run from someone."

As the conversation continued, it became clear that no one had concrete answers. The mystery of the stranger's death hung heavily over Maple Lake, and everyone seemed to be grasping at theories.

"I just hope the police can figure out what happened soon," I said, my voice weary.

Jake nodded in agreement. "Me too. For now, let's try to focus on the festival. We've worked so hard to make it a success, and it would be a shame to let this ruin it."

With that, the group began to disperse, each person lost in their own thoughts. Despite the damper the tragedy had on the festivities, there was only an hour before the festival would open for the day.

As the morning wore on, the town began to return to its normal rhythm, albeit with a palpable sense of apprehension. I went about my day trying to maintain a sense of normalcy.

Chapter 3

CHIEF MONROE

"Hey, Molly," Chief Monroe's voice rang out from the front of the inn as I finished pouring coffee for Lila and Jake and some lingering guests. The autumn sun hadn't fully risen yet, but he was already on the move, clipboard in hand, his expression a mix of professionalism and frustration. That last part was familiar. The chief had a way of making you feel like you were a hair away from meddling, which, in my case, wasn't too far from the truth.

I waved him in, knowing full well why he was there. The whole town knew. The body discovered behind the festival tents had thrown Maple Lake into a frenzy, and as much as I wanted to keep to myself, there was no avoiding the fact that I'd found the body. Along with Jake, of course. The town was already buzzing with rumors, but now, Chief Monroe had to sift through it all.

"Chief," I greeted as he stepped inside, his eyes already scanning the room, taking stock of everyone present. He was tall, with a gray patch of hair at his temples and the kind of weathered look you only get after years of dealing with small-town disputes and the occasional crime. Today, though, he looked more serious than usual.

"Cute dog." He broke character and referred to Mitz who seemed to hear the compliment and looked happier.

"Molly," he nodded, then glanced at Lila and Jake. "I'm going to need to ask some questions about what happened two days ago."

I gestured to the table. "Of course, Chief. Coffee?"

"Uh, thanks," he said gruffly, though his eyes softened a bit at the offer. He wasn't unkind, just... cautious. Especially when it came to me. He'd learned from the last case that I had a habit of getting involved, and he wasn't too keen on that happening again. But despite his gruff exterior, I knew he respected my instincts. Even if he wouldn't admit it.

He pulled up a chair, flipping open his notepad. "So, let's start from the beginning. You found the body with Jake?"

I nodded, sitting down across from him. "Yeah. We were coming home from the festival when Mitz here heard something. At first, I thought it was just the wind, but then we heard it again—a thud. Jake went to check it out, and I followed him. That's when we found the man behind the tent."

The chief scribbled a few notes. "And you didn't recognize him?"

"No," I said. "He wasn't from around here. He looked out of place. Have you been able to identify him?"

Chief Monroe sighed, rubbing his temples. "No. He didn't have any identification on him. It's as if he appeared out of nowhere. We have been able to confirm that the man's death is a homicide. We're still waiting on the forensics off the knife, but preliminary reports show no prints on it."

He glanced at Jake, who was leaning against the counter, arms crossed, listening intently. "And you? You didn't see anyone else? No suspicious activity during the festival?"

Jake shook his head. "It was quiet by the time we found him. Most folks had already gone home."

Chief Monroe's pen tapped against his notepad. "Alright. And no one else saw or heard anything strange?"

Lila, who had been uncharacteristically quiet, spoke up. "I didn't see anything, but I did hear some people talking earlier in the day about a man hanging around the festival that no one seemed to recognize."

"Who was talking?" Monroe asked, his eyes narrowing slightly.

Lila bit her lip, thinking. "Mrs. Jenkins, I think. And Clara from The Maple Mug. They were gossiping about him by the cider stand. Something about him looking a little too... secretive."

Monroe jotted that down, then flipped to a fresh page in his notepad. "I'll need to talk to them both. Thanks, Lila."

Lila nodded, her eyes darting to me. I could tell she was thinking the same thing I was—this wasn't going to be an open-and-shut case.

As Chief Monroe closed his notebook, I could see the gears turning in his head. "And Molly," he added, his voice taking on a more serious tone, "I need you to leave this one to me. I know how you get when something's off, but we've got this under control. The last thing we need is you getting involved again."

I opened my mouth to protest, but before I could say anything, the door to the inn swung open, and in walked Max, looking more disheveled than I'd ever seen him.

Max was usually so put together—his pet store always spotless, his clothes neat. But today, his shirt was wrinkled, and his face had a nervous energy to it that I hadn't seen before.

"Max!" I said, trying to hide my surprise. "What brings you here so early?"

He glanced around the room, his eyes landing briefly on Chief Monroe before shifting away. "I—I heard what happened. About the body. Is it true?"

Chief Monroe eyed him closely. "Yeah, it's true. But I don't think it's any of your concern."

Max shifted uncomfortably, running a hand through his messy hair. "Right. Of course. I just... I heard some of the townsfolk talking, and I wanted to make sure everything was... handled."

The chief leaned back in his chair, folding his arms. "Handled how?"

"I—uh..." Max hesitated, his eyes flicking toward the floor. "I don't know. I guess I just mean... if there's anything I can do to help..."

I frowned. Max was usually so calm, so composed. This jittery behavior didn't suit him at all. And from the look on Chief's face, he wasn't buying it either.

"We've got it under control, Max," Chief Monroe said, his voice a little sharper now. "Why don't you just go on about your business?"

Max swallowed hard, nodding quickly. "Yeah, sure. Of course."

Without another word, he turned and hurried out of the inn, the door closing a little too hard behind him.

Lila raised an eyebrow. "That was... weird."

Jake nodded. "He's been acting off lately. Even during the festival, I noticed he seemed distracted."

Chief Monroe glanced between us; his face was unreadable. "You think Max is involved in this?"

I shook my head slowly. "I don't know. It just doesn't feel like him. But something sure seems to be bothering him."

Chief Monroe didn't respond immediately. He just stood up, tucking his notepad back into his jacket. "I'll have a chat with Max, see what's going on. But in the meantime, Molly—stay out of it. I mean it this time."

I gave him a tight-lipped smile. "I'll do my best."

He narrowed his eyes, clearly not convinced, but he didn't push it further. As he headed out the door, I let out a sigh before turning to Jake and Lila.

"Well, that was interesting," Lila said, breaking the silence. "Max is acting strange. I've never seen him so nervous."

Jake nodded in agreement. "Yeah, he was fidgeting the whole time. And did you see how he barely looked Chief Monroe in the eye? That's not like him."

I stared at the door, my mind racing. Something wasn't adding up, and I could feel that familiar itch to dig deeper. Max had been acting off for days now, but I hadn't thought much of it until now. And if Chief Monroe wasn't going to take my hunches seriously...

"Molly," Jake said, his voice pulling me out of my thoughts. "You're thinking about getting involved, aren't you?"

I sighed, rubbing my hand over my face. "I don't know. I promised I'd stay out of it, but... something about this just feels wrong. And Max..."

Jake placed a hand on my shoulder. "Let's keep an eye on him, but don't stir the pot just yet. Let the police do their job for once."

Lila chimed in, her eyes twinkling with mischief. "But if something juicy comes up, you know I'll be right there with you. As for Max... well I'm already all over that."

I laughed despite myself. "Of course, you are."

But as I sat there, sipping my coffee and thinking about Max's strange behavior, I couldn't help but feel that this was just the beginning of something much bigger. Whatever secrets were lurking in Maple Lake, I had a feeling they were about to come to the surface. And whether Chief Monroe liked it or not, I was going to be right in the middle of it.

***

The rest of the day passed in a blur of whispers and rumors. Every time I stepped outside, someone else had a theory about what had happened or who the mysterious stranger might have been. By the time I made my way to the pet store later that afternoon, my head was spinning with all the possibilities. I just needed to see for myself what was up with Max.

The bell above the door jingled as I stepped inside, and there was Max, hunched over the counter, nervously tapping his fingers against the wood. He looked up when he saw me, his face pale.

"Molly," he said, his voice shaky. "What are you doing here?"

I gave him a friendly smile, though I was watching him closely. "Just thought I'd check in, see how you're holding up."

He forced a laugh, though it sounded more like a cough. "I'm fine. Just... you know, a little shaken up. That body and all..."

I leaned against the counter, studying him. "Max, are you sure everything's ok? You've been acting strange."

He shifted uncomfortably, avoiding my gaze. "I'm fine, really. Just... got a lot on my mind."

Before I could press him further, the door opened, and Chief Monroe walked in. He glanced at me briefly, showing no surprise that I was already questioning Max.

"Max," he said, his voice firm. "I need to ask you a few questions."

Max stiffened, his eyes widening slightly. "Of course, Chief. Anything you need.""Alone," the chief added, "Giving me a pointed look."

I reluctantly turned to leave as Chief Monroe began his questioning, but a familiar itch returned. Something was wrong here, and Max knew more than he was letting on. I just hoped I could figure it out before things got even worse.

Chapter 4

AN ARGUMENT

The late afternoon light filtered through the windows of the cozy kitchen where Lila and I sat sipping our tea in silence. The events of the past few days had been weighing heavily on us, and no matter how much we tried to make sense of it all, the pieces of the puzzle just didn't seem to fit. Mitz sat at our feet, playing with his chew toy.

I let out a sigh and placed my teacup down on the saucer, the clink of porcelain breaking the quiet. "Lila, I feel like we're missing something. There's got to be more to this than what we've seen so far."

Lila frowned, her brow creasing as she tucked her legs up under her on the chair. "I know what you mean. Max is acting strange, sure, but he's not the type to be involved in something this serious. Molly, you know I trust him. We're missing something, but it's not him."

I stared down at the table, my fingers tracing the wood grain as I thought back to the festival. We had been so busy with the guests at the inn, but there had been a few moments where I remembered seeing... something.

It hit me like a bolt of lightning. "Lila," I said, sitting up straighter, "do you remember when we were near the pie tent? Right before the festival started winding down?"

Lila's eyes narrowed as she thought back. "Yeah... we were in line to get a slice of Mrs. Pott's famous apple pie. Why?"

I leaned forward, lowering my voice as if sharing a secret. "Do you remember seeing Edith Patterson arguing with some man? She was at the booth next to us."

Lila's eyes widened in realization. "Oh my gosh, yes! I completely forgot about that. She was arguing with some man, but I didn't get a good look. Do you think it could have been the man who was found dead?"

We exchanged a look, the same thought dawning on both of us at once. "We need to think back to exactly what we overheard," I said, pushing aside my tea. "That conversation could be the key to all of this."

Lila set her cup down and leaned her elbows on the table. "Ok, let's piece it together. I remember we weren't paying full attention at first, but once their voices got louder, we couldn't help but listen."

I closed my eyes, trying to place myself back at the festival. The sounds of people laughing, the smell of pies baking, the hum of the crowd... and then, the sharp tone of an argument cutting through it all.

"It was Edith who raised her voice first," I recalled. "She was angry—really angry. I think it started with something about a payment?"

Lila snapped her fingers. "Yes! She said something like, 'I'm not going to pay you a cent more than we agreed on!' She was furious."

I nodded, the memory coming back more clearly now. "And the man—he didn't back down. He said something about her owing him more than just money, that she'd promised him something."

Lila bit her lip, thinking. "Right, and Edith... oh! She said some-thing like, 'I don't care what you think I owe you. This is my event, and you're not going to ruin it with your demands.'"

I could practically hear the tension in Edith's voice, the way it had risen over the noise of the festival. "That's when things got even more heated," I added. "The man stepped closer to her, and I remember feeling like something wasn't right."

A shiver ran down my spine as I remembered the cold edge in his voice. "And Edith... she didn't back down. She just glared at him and said, 'You don't scare me. Now get out of my sight before I call the police.'"

There was a long silence as we both sat there, the weight of what we'd overheard settling between us.

"Molly," Lila said quietly, "that wasn't that long before the people started to leave... before he was found dead. What if... what if Edith had something to do with it?"

I chewed my lip, thinking it over. Edith was tough, no doubt about it, and clearly capable of holding her own in an argument. But could she really be involved in something as serious as murder?

"It's possible," I said slowly. "But we need to be sure before we go pointing fingers. What we overheard makes her a suspect, but we don't have proof."

Nodding, Lila's expression was serious. "Right. But it's absolutely something Chief Monroe needs to know about. Maybe he can get more out of Edith than we could."

"I agree," I said, pushing back my chair and standing up. "We need to go talk to him."

Lila stood as well, grabbing her coat from the hook by the door. "Do you think he'll believe us? I mean, we didn't hear the whole conversation, just bits and pieces."

I shrugged, slipping on my jacket. "He might not believe us right away, but it's better than sitting here doing nothing. Besides, he knows we've got good instincts. Even if he doesn't want to admit it."

The cozy, familiar surroundings of Maple Lake felt strangely eerie now, like the picturesque charm of the town was hiding something darker beneath the surface.

When we reached the station, we found Chief Monroe at his desk, looking through some paperwork. He glanced up as we entered, his expression hardening slightly when he saw us.

"Molly, Lila," he said, setting down his pen. "What brings you here?"

I took a deep breath and stepped forward. "Chief, we need to talk to you about something we overheard at the festival."

Monroe raised an eyebrow, leaning back in his chair. "Overheard, huh? This wouldn't have anything to do with you sticking your nose where it doesn't belong again, would it?"

I shot him a look but kept my voice steady. "This is important, Chief. It's about Edith—the festival organizer. She was having a heated argument with the man who was murdered. Jake and I found his body shortly after. We think it might be relevant."

Chief Monroe's expression shifted slightly, a hint of interest replacing the skepticism. "Go on."

Lila and I took turns explaining the argument we'd overheard, recounting every detail we could remember. As we spoke, his face grew more serious. By the time we finished, he was leaning forward in his chair, his notepad open in front of him.

"So, you're telling me that Edith was threatening this guy?" he asked, scribbling down notes.

"Not exactly," I said. "But it was obvious that she wasn't happy with him. And he made an incredibly strong threat before walking away."

Monroe nodded slowly, his pen tapping against the notepad. "Alright. I'll have a chat with Edith. See if I can get her side of the story."

He looked up at us, his gaze sharp. "But I'm warning you both—stay out of this from here on out. I appreciate the information, but the last thing I need is for you two to get involved any further. Understand?"

Lila and I exchanged a look before nodding. "We understand, Chief," I said, trying to keep my voice neutral.

Chapter 5

EDITH

The morning fog had barely lifted when Lila and I found ourselves back in the kitchen, racking our brains over everything that had happened. Chief Monroe had been going around questioning half the town, but so far, it seemed like everyone had an alibi or an excuse. Still, there was one person I couldn't shake from my mind—Edith.

I poured another cup of coffee and sat down across from Lila. She was flipping through her notebook, where she had jotted down notes on everything we knew so far. "What if we're missing something obvious?" she muttered, her brow furrowed in concentration.

"We are," I said, tapping my finger against the side of my mug. "Remember the festival? Edith had that argument with him. It wasn't just casual, Lila. She was furious, and I can't help but think that's important."

Lila looked up with wide eyes. She leaned forward, her voice dropping to a conspiratorial whisper. "We need to go over that conversation again."

***

The memory of the argument at the Maple Lake Harvest Festival came rushing back to me. The air had been filled with the smell of caramel apples and roasted nuts, laughter and music echoing across the park. I hadn't thought much of it at the time, but now, every word Edith said felt heavy with meaning.

We had been near the pie contest booth when we heard it. Edith was in a heated discussion with the stranger, her voice low but seething. She didn't notice us as we passed by, but we couldn't help overhearing bits and pieces of their conversation.

"You think you can just come back here after all this time and act like nothing happened?" Edith's voice was sharp, almost venomous.

The stranger had remained calm, his voice low and steady. "It's not what you think. I'm not here to stir up trouble."

"You're nothing but trouble," Edith had shot back. "And if you think people around here have forgotten what you did, you're dead wrong."

Lila and I had exchanged a quick glance, both of us sensing the tension but not wanting to get involved at the time. I remembered how Edith had stormed off after that, her face red. The stranger stood there in her wake, looking frustrated but not surprised.

***

Now, sitting in the kitchen with Lila, I replayed the conversation in my head. "She was so angry," I said. "And now she's been absent, like she's trying to distance herself from the whole thing. That's not just a coincidence."

Lila nodded, her pen tapping against the notebook. "We need to talk to her. Get her to open up about what that argument was really about."

I sighed, knowing that confronting Edith wasn't going to be easy. She wasn't exactly known for being forthcoming, especially when it came to her personal business. But if we wanted answers, we had no choice.

***

Later that afternoon, we found Edith at the festival but not in her usual spot—she was sitting in the back of one of the tents just sipping apple cinnamon tea, watching the world go by. As we approached, she glanced up, her eyes narrowing slightly.

"Edith, there you are, we've been looking all over for you."

"Molly, Lila," she greeted us, her tone polite but guarded. "What brings you by?"

I forced a smile, trying to keep things light. "Just thought we'd check in. With everything going on, we wanted to see how you were doing."

Edith's eyes flickered with suspicion, but she gestured for us to sit. "I'm fine," she said, her voice clipped. "But why do I feel like this isn't just a social visit?"

I exchanged a quick look with Lila before speaking. "Actually, we wanted to talk about something we overheard the other day. Between you and the stranger.

Edith stiffened at the mention of the argument, her lips pressing into a thin line. "I don't know what you're talking about," she said flatly, but her eyes betrayed her. There was something there—guilt, maybe fear—barely hidden beneath the surface.

"We overheard you," Lila said gently, leaning forward. "You were upset with him. You said something about how people hadn't forgotten what he did. Edith, what was that about?"

For a moment, Edith just stared at us, her fingers gripping the edge of her teacup. The silence stretched, thick and tense, until she let out a slow breath, her shoulders sagging. "It's complicated," she muttered, her gaze dropping to the floor.

"Complicated how?" I pressed, keeping my voice calm but firm. "We're just trying to understand what's going on. Whatever you're not telling us, Edith, it might be important."

Her eyes flashed up at me, sharp and defensive. "I'm not hiding anything!" she snapped, but then caught herself, her expression softening. "Look, I didn't have anything to do with... what happened to him. But I'll admit, there's history between us. Old, ugly history."

Lila and I exchanged a quick glance. We were getting somewhere.

"What kind of history?" I asked, keeping my tone neutral.

Edith sighed and set her teacup down on the bench with a clink. "He wasn't always a stranger around here, you know. Years ago—back before any of this—he lived here. Different name back then, Ronald Waverly, but it was him. Caused quite a bit of trouble before he disappeared."

My heart skipped a beat. The stranger wasn't a stranger after all.

"I knew it," Lila whispered. "But what kind of trouble are we talking about, Edith?"

Edith hesitated, biting her lip as she considered her words. "He... he was involved with someone. A woman here in town. They had a nasty breakup—real nasty. Accusations flew. The whole thing got out of hand, and in the end, he left town. I thought that was the end of it."

I narrowed my eyes. "And when he showed up again, you confronted him?"

Edith nodded, her expression hardening. "I didn't want him here. His presence stirred up old wounds, things that people had tried to forget. I told him he wasn't welcome—that if he stayed, he'd only cause more problems. He didn't listen."

Lila spoke up, her voice careful. "What did he do to make you so sure he'd stir up trouble?"

Edith met Lila's gaze; her eyes were cold. "It wasn't just about the woman. He had a way of getting involved in other people's business. Sticking his nose where it didn't belong. He was good at getting under your skin—pushing buttons. He knew things about people, and he wasn't afraid to use that against them."

I felt a chill run down my spine. "So, you threatened him?"

Edith's jaw clenched. "I warned him, yes. But I didn't kill him, Molly. I wasn't the only one who had a reason to want him gone."

"Who else?" I asked, feeling the knot in my stomach tighten.

Edith glanced away, her fingers twisting in her lap. "There were others. People he'd wronged. You'd be surprised how many folks have skeletons in their closets, and he knew where most of them were buried."

The conversation had taken a dark turn, and I could feel the weight of it pressing down on us. Edith was holding back, but the truth was starting to slip through the cracks. Ronald Waverly, or whoever he is now, had stirred up something dangerous—something that had come back to haunt him.

"Edith," Lila said softly, "if there's more that you're not telling us, now's the time. We're trying to help."

Edith's eyes flickered with something like fear, but she shook her head. "I've told you everything I know. I didn't want him dead—I just wanted him gone. Now, if you'll excuse me, I think this conversation is over."

We stood reluctantly, knowing we wouldn't get anything else out of her for now. As we made our way out of the tent and back into the crowded festival, the weight of her words hung over us like a storm cloud.

***

"She's hiding something," Lila muttered as we walked. "I can feel it."

"I know," I replied. "But whatever it is, she's not ready to admit it. We'll have to keep digging."

We walked in silence for a while, both of us lost in thought. Edith's story had added more pieces to the puzzle, but it had also raised more questions. Who was this stranger, really? What had he done to make so many people want him gone?

"Do you think Chief Monroe knows about all this?" Lila asked suddenly, breaking the silence.

I shook my head. "I doubt it. Edith would never admit this to him, not without being forced to. She's too proud."

"So, what do we do now?"

I sighed, feeling the weight of the investigation pressing down on my shoulders. "We keep asking questions. Someone in this town knows more than they're letting on. And if Edith's right, there are more people with reasons to want him dead. We just have to figure out who."

Chapter 6

DENNIS

The next morning, I was sitting at my usual spot in the dining room, sipping coffee and staring out the window at the quiet street. Maplewood Haven had a way of feeling deceptively peaceful, even when there was a storm brewing just beneath the surface. And right now, that storm had a name: Dennis. He was the festival's security manager.

I had spent the better part of the evening rehashing everything we'd learned so far. Edith's cryptic comments, the stranger's murky past, and most notably, Dennis. He was always around—a reliable enough guy who kept to himself for the most part. But something had been off with him that night.

I was still mulling it over when Lila came in. "You're up early," she said.

"Couldn't sleep," I muttered, wrapping my hands around the warm mug. "Too much on my mind."

"Same here," she replied, sitting across from me.

"I can't stop thinking about Dennis. How come he wasn't there when we found the body. He should have been there. Something's not adding up. We need to talk to him."

"You're right. Where was he. After all security was his job. You think he'll talk?" Lila raised an eyebrow.

I shrugged. "It's worth a try. People tend to slip up when they're nervous."

We finished our coffee in silence, both of us lost in thought. There was something about Dennis that didn't sit right with me, and I had a gut feeling that if we dug deep enough, we'd find out what it was.

By mid-morning, we were heading over to the community center, where Dennis was supposed to be overseeing the festival. The center was bustling with activity. But Dennis was nowhere to be found.

Lila and I exchanged a glance. "Let's ask around," she suggested.

We approached one of the volunteers, a middle-aged woman named Cheryl who always had her ear to the ground when it came to local gossip.

"Hey, Cheryl," I said, smiling warmly. "Have you seen Dennis around? We wanted to talk to him."

Cheryl looked up from the folding chairs she was straightening and frowned. "Dennis? I saw him earlier this morning, but he disappeared about an hour ago. Said he had something to take care of but didn't say what."

Lila and I exchanged another look—this time with raised eyebrows.

"Did he seem off to you?" Lila asked, lowering her voice slightly.

Cheryl paused, thinking it over. "Well, now that you mention it, yeah. He was acting a little strange. Seemed distracted. Kept looking over his shoulder like he was expecting someone."

My stomach twisted. "Did he say where he was going?"

"Nope. Just said he'd be back later."

"Thanks, Cheryl," I said, forcing a smile. "Let us know if you see him."

We walked away, heading back outside where the cool autumn air greeted us. Lila was biting her lip, clearly thinking hard.

"He's definitely up to something," she muttered. "But what?"

"I don't know," I replied. "But I think it's time we had a little chat with Chief Monroe."

***

We found Chief Monroe at the station, sitting behind his cluttered desk, going through some paperwork. He looked up as we entered, his expression stern as always.

"Molly, Lila," he said, setting his pen down. "What brings you two here? Still poking around, I assume?"

I couldn't help but smile at his dry tone. Chief Monroe always pretended to be annoyed by our involvement in these investigations, but deep down, I knew he appreciated the help—especially when it led to a break in the case.

"We've got a lead," I said, pulling up a chair. "It's about Dennis. The security manager."

Chief Monroe's eyes narrowed. "What about him?"

"He's acting strange since the murder," Lila chimed in. "Cheryl said he left the festival this morning without explaining why. He's not where he's supposed to be, and it's not the first time."

Chief Monroe leaned back in his chair, folding his arms across his chest. "You're saying he's suspicious because he left work early?"

"No, it's more than that," I insisted. "Think about it. Where was he when this guy was murdered. He should have been at the festival grounds. He would have been the first to hear what we heard and yet he wasn't there. We got there first the night of the murder."

Chief Monroe's expression darkened. "If his whereabouts are unaccounted for; Yes, that changes things."

"We need to know more," Lila said. "Maybe he has a good explanation."

Chief sighed, rubbing his temples. "Alright. I'll check it out. But you two need to stay away. If Dennis is involved in this, you don't want to be poking the bear."

"Understood," I said, standing up. "But don't worry about us. We're just following the breadcrumbs."

***

It didn't take long for Chief Monroe to dig up some dirt on Dennis. As it turned out, he had a record—nothing major, but enough to raise some eyebrows. A few run-ins with the law in his younger days, mostly for petty theft and disorderly conduct. But there was one incident that caught my attention: a bar fight years ago that had gotten out of hand, resulting in serious injuries. Dennis had been charged with assault, though the case was eventually dropped.

When Chief Monroe filled us in, my mind started racing. Could Dennis have a violent streak?

"We need to talk to him," I said, pacing his office. "He's hiding something, and we need to find out what it is."

Chief Monroe nodded, already reaching for his jacket. "Ok, I'll let you tag along but stay out of the way. Let's go."

***

We found Dennis at his house, a small, run-down cottage on the edge of town. He looked surprised to see us, and his face quickly hardened when he saw Chief Monroe with us.

"What's this about?" Dennis asked, crossing his arms defensively.

"We need to talk," Chief Monroe said calmly. "It's about the night of the murder."

Dennis's jaw tightened. "What about it? I was at home."

Chief Monroe didn't miss a beat. "But you were on duty at the festival. You should have been at the grounds, Dennis. Care to explain why you weren't there?"

Dennis's face paled, and for a moment, I thought he was going to bolt. But instead, he just shook his head, his shoulders slumping.

"I didn't kill him," he muttered, running a hand through his hair. "I swear, I didn't."

"Then why the disappearing act?" Chief Monroe pressed, his tone firmer now.

Dennis hesitated, glancing between Monroe, Lila, and me. "I... I've got a record. Nothing serious, but I've been in trouble before. I didn't want anyone pointing fingers at me."

"That's not good enough," Chief Monroe said. "You need to tell us the truth."

Dennis let out a shaky breath, his eyes darting nervously. "Alright, fine. I wasn't at home. I was... I was meeting someone that night. Someone I didn't want anyone to know about."

"Who?" I asked, my heart pounding in my chest.

Dennis clenched his fists, his gaze dropping to the ground. "I can't say. But I swear, it had nothing to do with the murder."

Chief Monroe stepped closer, his voice low and menacing. "If you're protecting someone, now's the time to come clean, Dennis. Otherwise, things are going to get a lot worse for you."

Dennis didn't say anything, but the fear in his eyes told me all I needed to know. He was hiding something—and whoever he was protecting might be the key to solving this case.

Chapter 7

EDITH'S SECRET

Lila and I exchanged a look before knocking on Edith's door. It had been only a couple of days since we last talked to her, but something didn't sit right with us. Edith had been defensive, and I couldn't shake the feeling that there was more to the story—more to her connection with the Ronald Waverly.

The door creaked open, revealing Edith's tired, pale face. Her hair was disheveled, and she looked like she hadn't slept since we last saw her. The bags under her eyes told a story of their own.

"Molly... Lila," she greeted us, her voice sounding flat and exhausted. "Now what?"

I forced a smile. "We just have a few more questions, Edith. We're not trying to upset you, but there are still some gaps in the story we need to fill in."

Edith hesitated, but then she stepped aside, allowing us to enter. We walked into the small living room where the smell of old coffee hung in the air. It was cluttered, with papers and books scattered across the coffee table, as though Edith had been deep in thought—or maybe deep in worry.

She sank into her armchair with a sigh, motioning for us to sit. Lila and I sat down across from her, the atmosphere thick with tension.

"So," Edith began, rubbing her hands together nervously, "what do you want to know now?"

Lila leaned forward slightly. "We know there was an argument between you and Ronald shortly before he was killed. We just need you to be honest with us, Edith. What was that argument about?"

For a moment, Edith was silent, her eyes flicking between Lila and me. Her lips pressed into a thin line, and I could see the battle waging inside her—whether to trust us or to keep her walls intact.

Finally, she sighed deeply, as though giving up on whatever she had been holding in. "I might as well tell you," she muttered, more to herself than to us. "But you have to promise... no one else can know."

"We can't make promises like that, Edith," I said gently. "If it's related to the murder, Chief Monroe will need to know."

Edith clenched her hands into fists on her lap. "I know. I just... this is something I've been keeping buried for years."

Lila gave her a soft, reassuring look. "It's Ok, Edith. Take your time."

Edith took a deep breath, her voice trembling as she began. "It wasn't just a simple argument. It was... it was about blackmail."

Lila and I exchanged a quick glance.

"Blackmail?" I echoed, trying to keep my voice calm. "What did he have on you?"

Edith's eyes filled with tears. "It was years ago. I made a mistake. A stupid, terrible mistake." She swallowed hard. "He found out about it and... he used it against me."

Lila's voice was gentle but probing. "What mistake, Edith?"

She wiped her eyes with the back of her hand. "It was a business deal—an investment. I got involved with some people I shouldn't have. I was desperate at the time, and they promised quick returns. But it turned out to be a scam, and I lost everything."

My heart sank as I listened to her. Edith had always been a proud woman, always in control. To hear her admit to something like this was heartbreaking.

"But the worst part," she continued, "was that I didn't just lose my own money. I convinced others in the town to invest as well. People trusted me. They believed in me. And when the deal fell apart... they lost everything too. They just don't know it; I couldn't bring myself to tell them. All this time they assumed the investment was collecting interest. I thought I would be able to find a way to pay everyone back, but..."

I leaned forward, trying to piece it all together. "And Ronald—he knew about this?"

Edith nodded, her hands trembling. "Yes. He found out. I don't know how, but he did. He came to me a few years ago and said he'd keep quiet if I paid him. I didn't have a choice. I couldn't let anyone find out, not after everything I'd done."

Lila's brow furrowed. "So, you've been paying him for years?"

Edith nodded again; her face contorted in shame. "I didn't have a choice. Every month, he'd show up, and I'd have to hand over the money. And every time, I felt like I was losing a piece of myself, and any chance of being able to compensate the investors."

My mind raced as I processed what she was telling us. Blackmail. A secret Edith had been carrying for years. It explained so much—the tension, the fear, the defensiveness. But it also raised more questions.

"What happened the night of the murder?" I asked gently. "What did you argue about?"

Edith's face darkened. "He wanted more. More money. I told him I couldn't keep doing it. I was running out of money, and I was tired of living in fear. I told him it had to stop."

"And what did he say?" Lila asked, her voice soft but firm.

Edith's lips trembled. "He laughed. He said if I didn't pay up, he'd ruin me. He'd go to the press, tell everyone in town what I'd done. My whole life would have been over."

I exchanged a look with Lila. It was starting to make sense now—the anger, the desperation. But something still didn't fit.

"And after the argument?" I asked. "What happened?"

"I told him to leave. I told him I wouldn't give him another penny." Edith's voice cracked. "He said I'd regret it. But I didn't care anymore. I just wanted it to be over."

"And then?" Lila prompted.

Edith took a deep breath, her voice barely above a whisper. "He left. I didn't see him again after that. The next thing I heard... he was dead."

The room fell silent, the weight of her words hanging in the air. Lila and I sat there, absorbing the shock of what she had told us. Blackmail. Threats. Desperation. Edith had been pushed to her breaking point, but that didn't necessarily mean she had killed him.

"Edith," I said softly, "I know this has been incredibly difficult for you. But you need to tell Chief Monroe the truth. He needs to hear this from you."

Her eyes filled with fear. "Do you think he'll believe me?"

I hesitated, unsure how to answer. "I don't know. But if you keep this a secret, it's only going to make things worse. You need to be honest."

Lila nodded in agreement. "You're not the only one with a motive, Edith. There are other people in this town with secrets—people who might have had their own reasons for wanting him dead."

Edith's face crumpled, and she buried her head in her hands. "I don't know what to do. I feel like my whole world is falling apart."

"We'll help you," I said firmly. "But you need to trust us. We need to get ahead of this before it gets any worse."

She looked up at me, her eyes red and swollen. "I'll do it. I'll talk to Chief Monroe."

I reached out and placed a hand on her shoulder. "You're doing the right thing."

As Lila and I stood up to leave, Edith followed us to the door, her face still etched with worry. I could only hope that by coming forward, she'd be able to clear her name—or at least stop living in fear.

"I just hope this doesn't make things worse," Edith whispered as we stepped outside.

Chapter 8

MAX

I couldn't help but notice how quiet Max had become. Ever since the investigation into Ronald's death began, his behavior had shifted from friendly and open to distracted and secretive. Every time I saw him around town, he seemed more on edge, avoiding eye contact, and keeping his head down.

Lila and I sat at Maplewood Haven's kitchen table, sipping our coffee and going over what we knew so far. The investigation was dragging on, and each day felt longer than the last. The air in town was thick with tension, and gossip about the murder was spreading like wildfire.

"Do you think Max is hiding something?" Lila asked, voicing the thought that had been lingering in my mind for days.

I sighed, stirring my coffee absentmindedly. "I don't know. But his behavior lately... it's off. He's been acting strange ever since the body was found."

Lila nodded, leaning back in her chair. "He used to have fun with me all the time, but now he barely says two words when I see him. We were good and now I feel like I'm losing him."

"Maybe it's just stress," I said, trying to give him the benefit of the doubt. "He's such a perfectionist with his shop; not to mention this whole situation has everyone on edge."

"True," Lila agreed. "But it feels like more than that. He's been avoiding everyone, not just me. And did you see how he reacted when Chief Monroe questioned him? He looked like a deer caught in the headlights."

I nodded. "I noticed that too. But to be fair, Chief Monroe can be intimidating."

Lila chuckled softly. "Yeah, especially when he's in full-on investigator mode."

We both fell silent for a moment, the only sound in the kitchen being the soft clink of our coffee cups against the table. My mind was racing, trying to piece together what we knew about Max and why he was acting so strangely.

I broke the silence. "He's normally so eager to talk about his plans for the pet store. Lately he barely talks at all."

Lila frowned. "I noticed that too. He was so excited with everything going so well at the store, but lately, it's like he's a whole different person. He seemed oddly excited about this festival and now we haven't even gone. It's been two weeks since he's taken me on a date."

I stared out the window, watching the light drizzle of rain falling outside. Something about Max just didn't add up. And the more I thought about it, the more certain I became that he was hiding something.

"We need to talk to him," I said finally. "Ask him what's going on."

Lila raised an eyebrow. "And what do we say? 'Hey Max, we think you're acting weird, are you hiding something?'"

I laughed despite myself. "Ok, maybe not exactly like that. But we could ask him how he's doing, see if he'll tell us anything."

Lila took a sip of her coffee, thinking it over. "It's worth a shot. But if he's hiding something, he might not be too keen on talking."

I shrugged. "It's better than sitting here and doing nothing."

Later that afternoon, we headed over to Max's pet store. The bell above the door jingled as we stepped inside, and the familiar smell of hay and small animals hit me. The shop was quiet, and Max was behind the counter, fiddling with something on the computer.

When he looked up and saw us, his expression shifted for just a moment—an almost imperceptible flicker of discomfort—before he forced a smile.

"Molly, Lila," he greeted us, his voice overly cheerful. "What are you two up to today?"

I glanced at Lila, who gave me a subtle nod. Time to dive in.

"Hey, Max," I said casually, leaning against the counter. "We just wanted to check in. How are things going?"

Max's smile faltered, and he glanced down at the counter, avoiding eye contact. "Things are fine. Busy, you know."

Busy? The shop was practically empty, and with the festival going on, it had been that way for days. Something wasn't right.

"We've noticed you've been a bit quiet lately," Lila chimed in, her tone gentle. "Everything ok?"

Max's eyes darted between us, and for a moment, he seemed unsure of how to respond. Finally, he let out a nervous chuckle. "I guess with everything going on it's been a bit distracting around here."

I tilted my head, watching him closely. "You mean the investigation?"

He nodded, but it felt like there was more to it than that. "Yeah, I mean... a murder in town and now all the publicity with the festival; so many visitors hearing about it? That's not exactly good for business, you know?"

Lila and I exchanged a look. Sure, a murder could affect business, but Max was acting like there was something more at play.

"Is that all that's bothering you?" Lila asked, her voice soft but probing.

Max hesitated, his fingers tapping nervously on the counter. "I—yeah. I mean, what else would it be?"

His response was too quick, too defensive. Something was off.

Lila leaned forward slightly, keeping her tone light. "It's just that... you seem a bit more rattled than everyone else. If something's going on, you can talk to me."

Max's eyes widened for a moment, and I saw the panic flash across his face. But then he quickly composed himself, forcing another smile.

"I appreciate that," he said, his voice tight. "But really, everything's fine. Just dealing with the usual stress, you know, store stuff. Chief wants me to come by later. He's got some questions, I guess but..."

Before we could press him further, the bell over the door jingled again, and a customer walked in. Max seemed relieved by the interruption, quickly turning his attention to the new arrival.

Lila and I took the hint. We waved goodbye to Max and left the shop.

Chapter 9

MAX'S INTERROGATION

I made my way to Chief Monroe's office. The investigation was still dragging on, and with each passing day, the tension only seemed to grow. People were on edge, and the usual sense of community that Maple Lake was known for was starting to fray around the edges. Max's odd behavior was the talk of the town, and now it was Chief Monroe's turn to question him directly.

Lila had stayed back at The Haven to help with the guests, but I wanted to be there when Chief Monroe questioned Max. Not because I didn't trust the chief—he was a good cop, thorough and by the book—but because something about Max's behavior gnawed at me. I had to hear it for myself. I needed to know why he'd been acting so distant.

As I stepped into the office, Chief Monroe was already seated behind his desk, his expression as serious as ever. Max sat across from him, his foot tapping nervously against the wooden floor. When Max caught sight of me, a flicker of unease crossed his face, but he quickly masked it, offering a strained smile.

"Molly," Chief Monroe greeted me, gesturing to an empty chair beside Max. "You're just in time. We were about to get started."

I took my seat, feeling the weight of the moment settle over me. Max shifted in his chair, his hands clenched in his lap. It was obvious that he didn't want to be here, and I couldn't blame him. Being questioned by the police was never a pleasant experience.

"Max," Chief Monroe began, his voice calm but firm, "I've been hearing from quite a few people in town that you've been acting a bit... unusual lately. Care to explain what's going on?"

Max blinked, his gaze darting between me and Chief Monroe. "Unusual? I—I don't know what you mean."

Chief Monroe leaned back in his chair, folding his arms across his chest. "You've been keeping to yourself more, avoiding conversations, and from what I've been told, you seem on edge. It's understandable given what's been happening, but it's also raised some suspicions. Is there something you're not telling us?"

Max swallowed hard, his fingers drumming anxiously on the armrest. "I'm just... I've had a lot on my mind, ok? This whole murder investigation... it's not exactly great for business. People don't want to come to a town where there's been a murder."

Chief Monroe's eyes narrowed slightly, but he didn't press Max right away. Instead, he glanced down at his notes before looking back up at him.

"That may be true. Can you explain your whereabouts the night of the murder."

Max stiffened in his chair, his face paling slightly. "I—well, no one's asked, but I don't see how it's relative. Not sure it's anyone's business where I was. I didn't know the guy who was killed, and I wasn't even at the festival so why would anyone care where I was?"

Chief Monroe's lips tightened into a thin line. "You were the last person seen near the square that night, Max. Witnesses say they saw you closing up your shop later than usual."

Max's eyes widened, and he shook his head vehemently. "No! I mean, yes, I was there, but I wasn't doing anything wrong. I stayed late to do inventory at my store. I wasn't anywhere near where the body was found."

"Then why not just say that from the beginning?" Chief Monroe's voice was still calm, but there was an edge to it now.

Max hesitated, his gaze dropping to the floor. For a moment, the room was filled with a tense silence. I watched him closely, searching for any sign that he might be hiding something. His shoulders were hunched, his eyes downcast, and he acted more cornered than guilty.

"I am just trying to stay away from this. I didn't want anyone to get the wrong idea," Max finally said, his voice low. "You both know I've had some trouble in the past, and I know how people can be. They see you keeping to yourself, and suddenly you're a suspect. I didn't want that kind of attention, not with everything that's happened."

Chief Monroe leaned forward slightly, his eyes never leaving Max.

Max shifted again in his seat, the tension radiating off him like heat from a stove. "Look, this has nothing to do with this murder. I need to think about my store. I'm starting over here. It's been going great; seriously great. I like this town; I like the people. I just... need to leave my past in the past. I've been trying to stay away from trouble since then."

He gave me a nervous glance, then looked away, his jaw clenched. "It's not something I want to advertise, Molly. I'm not proud of it. I moved here to get a fresh start, to leave all that behind."

Chief Monroe was still watching Max closely, his expression unreadable.

Max hesitated again, visibly weighing his options before he sighed and ran a hand through his hair. "The way I see it, I almost died. I figure I did my time, paid my dues. But when something like this happens, people start to remember things and it's like I have to go through it all again."

Chief Monroe responded with a thoughtful tone. "That situation with the exotic animals wasn't your doing and I know you got wrapped up in it but it's not exactly murder. I can see why you'd be nervous about how it might look. Still, avoiding everyone isn't helping your case. If you're innocent, you need to be upfront with people."

Max nodded, but the tension in his body didn't ease. "I know, I know. I just didn't want people digging into my past. I've been trying to keep my head down, run my shop, and not cause any trouble."

Monroe leaned back in his chair, his eyes narrowing slightly. "We've checked out your whereabouts for that night, and while there's nothing that definitively places you at the scene of the crime, there's nothing that clears you either."

Max's face paled further, and he started to wring his hands. "I told you; I was doing inventory alone. I didn't leave the shop until after midnight. By then, everything had already happened."

Chief Monroe didn't say anything for a moment, letting the silence stretch between them. I could see chief wasn't getting anything from this conversation.

"Here's the thing, Max," Chief finally said, his voice calm but firm. "I want to believe you. But you've been acting suspiciously, and people in this town are starting to wonder if there's more to your story than you're letting on. If you're not guilty, now's the time to come clean about anything else you've been hiding."

Max's eyes flickered toward me again, a look of desperation in his expression. "I swear, I didn't kill that man. I don't know why he was here or what he was involved in, but I had nothing to do with it."

I believed him—at least, I wanted to. There was something about the way Max was acting that made me think he wasn't a killer. But there was no denying he was hiding something, something he wasn't ready to share yet.

Chief Monroe let out a long sigh, standing up and crossing his arms over his chest. "Max, we're going to keep digging. If there's more to find, we will, and if you are involved you're going to find yourself in deeper water than you would have been."

Max swallowed hard, nodding slightly. "I understand."

With that, Chief Monroe gave me a brief nod, signaling that the questioning was over. I rose from my chair, feeling the weight of the moment still pressing down on me. Max looked like he was about to crumble, his usual calm and collected demeanor shattered.

Chapter 10

MAYOR HARRISON

Mitz lay curled up on the couch, his little body rising and falling with each gentle breath. He hadn't stirred since I poured myself a second cup of coffee, and I envied his ability to sleep so peacefully amidst all this chaos.

I, on the other hand, couldn't seem to relax. My mind was running circles around itself, trying to piece together the events of the past week. First, Ronald Waverly shows up in town and then winds up dead under mysterious circumstances. Max had been acting weird ever since, and while he was clear for now, something still didn't sit right. There was more at play—something we were missing.

Jake walked in, freshly showered, his damp hair sticking up in all directions. He looked as tired as I felt, and I could tell the case had been keeping him up too.

"Molly," he said, pouring himself a cup of coffee and sitting down across from me at the small kitchen table. "I can't shake this feeling that we're looking in the wrong direction."

I nodded, staring down into my cup. "Max is acting strange, sure, but he doesn't feel like the killer. At least I believe him about this."

Jake took a long sip of his coffee, setting the mug down with a thud. "Exactly. He's hiding something, but it's not murder. What about the mayor? Vincent Harrison?"

That name caught me off guard. Mayor Harrison had been in office for as long as I could remember.

I glanced over at Mitz, who had perked up slightly, his big brown eyes watching me as if he, too, were waiting for answers.

"The mayor?" I asked, raising an eyebrow. "You really think he could be involved?"

Jake shrugged, leaning back in his chair. "I don't know, but something about him doesn't add up. I was talking to Carl at the hardware store yesterday, and he mentioned seeing the mayor talking to the stranger in the days leading up to the festival. They were arguing. Why has no one asked him about that yet?"

"Arguing?" I repeated, my interest piqued. "Why didn't we hear about this sooner?"

Jake sighed, running a hand through his hair. "Carl wasn't sure it was important. You know how he is—he doesn't like to stick his nose where it doesn't belong. But if Mayor Harrison was involved with the victim, even peripherally, we need to find out why."

I thought about it for a moment, my mind running through everything I knew about Mayor Harrison. He was clean-cut, well-liked, a bit of a showoff and some would say that he thought he owned the town, but he always appeared to have the town's best interest at heart. Then again, people like that were often the ones with the most to hide.

"What's the plan?" I asked, leaning forward.

Jake gave me a knowing look. "We start asking questions."

Mitz jumped down from the couch and trotted over to me, his tiny paws making soft tapping sounds against the hardwood floor. I leaned down to scratch behind his ears, and he let out a little yawn, as if the whole situation was exhausting him.

"You're coming too, boy," I told him with a smile. "Maybe people will be more willing to talk if they're distracted by your cuteness."

Jake chuckled, standing up and grabbing his jacket from the back of the chair. "Let's hope he's our secret weapon."

We headed out into the crisp morning air, Mitz trotting happily beside me, his leash clutched in my hand. As we walked through the town, I couldn't help but notice how quiet everything felt. The usual hum of Maple Lake seemed muted, as if the recent events had cast a shadow over the place.

Our first stop was the mayor's office. It was housed in an old brick building near the town square, the same building where countless town meetings had been held over the years. I had never felt nervous walking into the mayor's office before, but today was different. Today, we weren't just ordinary citizens—we were investigators.

Jake held the door open for me, and Mitz trotted in confidently, his nose twitching as he took in the smells of the office. The receptionist, a kind woman named Susan, looked up from her desk with a smile.

"Molly, Jake—what a pleasant surprise. What can I do for you two today?"

I smiled back, trying to keep things casual. "Hi, Susan. Is Mayor Harrison in? We just have a few questions we were hoping he could help us with."

Susan frowned slightly, her eyes flicking to the door behind her. "He's in a meeting right now, but I can let him know you're here. Is everything alright?"

Jake leaned against the counter, crossing his arms. "Nothing to worry about, Susan. We're just following up on some things related to the festival."

She nodded, picking up the phone and dialing a number. I could feel my palms sweating as I waited. Mitz nudged my leg with his nose, sensing my nerves.

After a few moments, Susan hung up the phone and smiled. "He'll be out in just a minute. Why don't you two take a seat?"

We thanked her and sat down in the small waiting area. Mitz hopped onto my lap and curled up. I absentmindedly scratched behind his ears, my mind racing. What were we going to ask him? How could we approach this without sounding accusatory?

Jake seemed calm; his eyes focused on the door to the mayor's office. He always had this way of staying level-headed in situations like these, and I was grateful for it.

A few minutes later, the door opened, and Mayor Harrison stepped out, his usual polished smile on his face. He was tall, with silver hair that gave him an air of authority, and his suit was as crisp as ever.

"Molly, Jake," he greeted us warmly, extending a hand to shake. "What brings you here today?"

I stood up, shifting Mitz to one arm as I shook his hand. "Mayor, we were hoping you could help us with something."

His smile faltered just slightly, but he quickly recovered. "Of course. What do you need to know?"

Jake stepped forward, his tone calm but firm. "We've heard from a few people around town that they saw you speaking with the victim in the days before his death. Some even said there was an argument. We were hoping you could shed some light on that."

The mayor's expression tightened, and for the first time, I saw a hint of unease in his eyes. "I did speak with him, yes. But I wouldn't call it an argument."

Mitz shifted on my arm, my gaze never leaving the mayor. "May we ask what the conversation was about?"

He cleared his throat, glancing at the receptionist briefly before motioning for us to follow him into his office. Once the door was closed behind us, he leaned against his desk, crossing his arms.

"The truth is the man came to me asking for help. He said he was in some kind of trouble—something to do with a deal gone wrong. I didn't get the details, but he seemed desperate. I told him there wasn't much I could do. I'm the mayor, not a private investigator."

Jake raised an eyebrow. "Did he mention what kind of deal it was?"

The mayor shook his head. "No, and I didn't ask. I didn't want to get involved. I told him to go to the police, but he refused. Said it wasn't something they could help with."

I exchanged a glance with Jake, my mind racing. A deal gone wrong. Could that have been what led to his death?

"Why didn't you tell the police about this after the murder?" I asked.

Mayor Harrison hesitated, his gaze flicking to the window. "I didn't think it was relevant. I made my public statement after the incident. I think this should be left to the police now. The man is dead—I didn't see how any conversation I had with him would change anything."

"That's for the police to decide," Jake said, his tone firm. "You should have told them."

The mayor sighed, rubbing a hand over his face. "I suppose you're right. I didn't want to drag myself into something that could harm my reputation."

Ah, there it was—the polished mayor, always thinking about his image. It didn't surprise me, but it certainly made me question if there was something he might be hiding.

Mitz let out a little bark, and I glanced down at him, smiling despite the tension. He always seemed to know when to break the ice.

Mayor Harrison's expression softened as he looked at Mitz, and he gave a small chuckle. "Cute dog. I could use a little distraction right about now."

I smiled back, trying to keep things light. "He's good at that."

Jake cleared his throat, bringing the conversation back on track. "Mayor, is there anything else you can tell us about the man? Anything at all that might help with the investigation?"

The mayor shook his head, his expression serious. "No, I'm afraid that's all I know. But I'll speak to the police if you think it will help."

I nodded, though I wasn't entirely convinced.

***

Mitz trotted beside me.

As we passed by the general store, Jake suddenly stopped and nodded toward the entrance. "Wait here for a sec."

Before I could ask why, he slipped inside. I stood there, a bit confused, as Mitz circled around my feet, his nose twitching at the scents carried by the breeze. A minute later, Jake emerged, holding something small in his hand.

"Here," he said, kneeling to offer the item to Mitz. His eyes lit up, his tail wagging furiously as he sniffed at the treat. Jake chuckled as Mitz carefully took the biscuit from his hand and immediately began to nibble on it, his tiny jaws working away with enthusiasm.

"He's spoiled," I teased, watching him happily munch away.

Jake stood back up, slipping his hands into his pockets. "He deserves it after the morning we've had. And... well, I thought he might like it."

"He does," I said softly, feeling warmth bloom in my chest. Jake had this way of surprising me—small gestures that showed how thoughtful he really was, beneath his usually stoic exterior.

When we reached the front of Maplewood Haven I paused, turning to Jake with a smile. "Thanks for today. I'm not sure I could've handled all this alone."

Jake met my eyes, his expression softening in a way that made my heart skip a beat. "You don't have to do this alone, Molly. You never have to."

There was something in the way he said it, a quiet intensity in his voice, that made me blush. I looked down, feeling my face grow warm, and was suddenly very aware of how close we were standing.

"I was actually thinking..." Jake began, rubbing the back of his neck like he always did when he was unsure of himself. "Maybe I could stay over tonight. I mean, with everything going on, it'd be better if I'm close. You know, just in case."

"Uh, yeah," I stammered, trying to sound casual. "That... that might be a good idea." I gave him a big silly grin.

Jake's lips curved into a small smile, and he took a step closer. "I just want to be here. With you."

And just like that, my heart was racing. I didn't trust myself to say anything without sounding like a flustered mess, so I simply nodded, my cheeks burning. Mitz, oblivious as always, let out a happy bark, as if giving his approval. We were dating and I was still acting like it was a crush.

Jake chuckled softly, the sound sending shivers down my spine. "Good," he said. "It's settled then."

Chapter 11

FESTIVAL LEADS

"Good morning, Jake." I beamed as I offered him a cup of coffee. "I'm not sure if I slept so well because I was exhausted or if I just felt safe with you nearby. Either way, thank you for staying last night. I needed a good night's rest."

"Absolutely, Molly. I think we all needed some good sleep. What's your plan for today after you finish up breakfast here?"

Lila bounced into the room eyeing us back and forth with a knowing smirk on her face. "Well, good morning to you *both*." She emphasized.

I ignored her comment. "Lila and I are headed back to the festival. I'm sure there's more to figure out, and I think being in the middle of it will be our best bet for finding more leads."

"Sounds like a plan. Keep me posted. I've got to get to the store, so I'll see you two later." Jake snatched a warm blueberry pancake with a wink and headed out.

"Ok, Molly you will need to fill me in on that later." Lila teased.

***

"Are you ready for some fun, Mitz?" I asked, giving him a scratch behind the ears. He barked in response as if to say he was ready for anything. "Let's get to the festival, buddy."

Lila and I wandered through the crowd, Mitz trotting happily beside us.

"Do you think the pumpkin carving contest will be as exciting as last year?" Lila asked, her eyes scanning the booths filled with handmade crafts and seasonal treats.

As we meandered through the bustling crowd, I noticed a group of locals gathered near the pie-eating contest. Their laughter momentarily distracted me from my worries. But then, drawn by an invisible force, my attention shifted to a small booth tucked away in the corner. It was manned by an elderly woman with kind eyes and a weathered face, selling antiques and trinkets.

"Let's check that out," I suggested, leading Lila toward the booth. Mitz, ever curious, darted ahead, sniffing at the various items displayed.

"Look at this," Lila said, picking up a delicate brooch shaped like a maple leaf. The copper hues caught the sunlight beautifully. "It's lovely."

I took the brooch from her, admiring the craftsmanship. "It must be quite old. I wonder who it belonged to."

Mitz's nose suddenly went on overload as he tugged the leash fiercely in the direction of the tent where the body had been found. "Whoa, Mitz, what's up with you this morning?"

He led us near the tent where his nose stopped on a flyer that had blown between a hay bale and the tent. Mitz wagged his tail happily as if he knew he found something.

"What is it, Molly?" Lila eyed me.

"It appears to be a real estate flyer. Look this up on your phone. Let's see if it means anything."

A quick Google search led us to a site for a real estate business. A business that had Mayor Harrison's name on it. My mind started swimming in questions. "This can't be a coincidence."

Lila nodded, her expression serious. "What do you think this means?"

"It means the mayor might be connected to more than he's letting on. We'll need to dig deeper."

Just then, a familiar face appeared among the festival-goers—Chief Monroe, looking as serious as ever. He was talking to a few townspeople, gesturing emphatically, his brows furrowed in concentration. I exchanged a glance with Lila, the same thought racing through our minds.

"We should ask him about the flyer and if he thinks the mayor's business may be linked to the victim," I whispered, my heart racing with curiosity and concern.

We approached the chief, who noticed us and straightened up. "Molly, Lila, what are you two up to today?"

"Just enjoying the festival," I replied, trying to keep my tone casual. "But Mitz just happened upon this flyer over near the tent where the victim was found. Do you think it has a connection?" I showed him the flyer, and he said he was sort of aware.

He hesitated, glancing around as if weighing his words. "Right now, I'm focused on gathering evidence. There's a lot we still don't know about that relationship."

"Do you think our mayor could actually be involved... in murder?" Lila asked, her voice cautious but tinged with urgency.

"I can't jump to conclusions, but there are certainly some troubling connections," he admitted, looking troubled. "Mayor Harrison and Ronald Waverly had dealings years ago, and I'm still piecing together the timeline."

"What kind of dealings?" I asked, leaning in closer.

The chief sighed, rubbing the back of his neck. "Nothing I can disclose at the moment, but I'll tell you this—whatever it was, it's raising some eyebrows."

I felt a shiver run down my spine. Before we could ask more questions, Mitz darted off.

"Wait up, Mitz!" He ran toward a nearby booth filled with old photographs and scrapbooks, his little nose leading him toward something.

"Come on, let's go," Lila said, following my lead.

As we approached the booth, an elderly man stood behind the table, displaying an array of photographs from years past. Mitz was sniffing eagerly at a stack of dusty old albums, his excitement contagious. I flipped through the pages, the faded images revealing snippets of Maple Lake's history.

"Wow, look at this," I said, pointing to a picture of a much younger Vincent Harrison standing alongside another man, their arms slung around each other's shoulders, both beaming. The man next to him had a familiar face—a face I recognized from the recent articles about the murder.

"Who's that?" Lila asked, leaning closer to get a better look. "He looks like Ronald Waverly."

"Yes! That's definitely him," I confirmed, feeling a sense of urgency. "What are the odds that they were friends?"

"Or more than friends," Lila added, her brows knitting together. "This could be the connection we've been looking for."

We continued flipping through the albums, uncovering more photographs of Vincent and Ronald together at various events, their camaraderie evident in every shot. Each image deepened my suspicions. I felt a strange mix of dread and intrigue, the pieces of a puzzle slowly revealing themselves.

"Maybe we should talk to some of the older townsfolk," I suggested, flipping through another album. "They might remember more about the mayor's past."

"Good idea," Lila replied. "We need to follow this lead. "Let's see if anyone here remembers their relationship."

Just then, Mitz darted toward a nearby crate, and I hurried after him. He was sniffing at something lying on the ground, his little tail wagging furiously. "What is it, Mitz?" I called out.

As I knelt beside him, I discovered it was a crumpled flyer for a charity event from several years ago. I picked it up, brushing off the dirt. The headline read "A Night for Maple Lake" with a list of sponsors that included Mayor Harrison's name prominently featured.

"Look at this," I said, showing Lila the flyer. "He was involved in this charity event. Why would this be laying here all crumpled up when it's from so long ago?"

Lila squinted at the fine print. "It says here they raised funds for local youth programs. What's that got to do with the victim?"

As we continued to dig, the festival activities swirled around us, but my focus was laser sharp. "We need to find out if there were any incidences or issues surrounding this event. It could provide insight into the mayor's old business dealings."

"Agreed," Lila said. "Let's ask around and see if anyone remembers the event."

We moved through the festival, and soon, I spotted a group of older women sitting at a table, knitting and chatting. Their laughter drew me in, and I decided to approach them, hoping they might remember something about the charity event.

"Excuse me, ladies," I said, smiling brightly. "Do you remember the charity event 'A Night for Maple Lake'? We're curious about how the mayor was involved with that."

One of the women, a petite lady with silver hair, perked up. "Oh, yes! That was a lovely evening. Vincent Harrison was quite the charmer. But I remember afterward there were some whispers about the money raised and how it was used."

"Whispers?" I asked, leaning closer.

"Rumors," she continued, glancing at her friends. "Some folks believed he was pocketing a portion of the donations. It raised eyebrows, and I know a few people who stopped attending after that."

My heart raced. "Did anyone confront him about it?"

Another woman shook her head. "Not directly. But there was a lot of gossip, and eventually, he seemed to avoid fundraisers. I always thought it was a shame."

I exchanged a look with Lila, excitement coursing through me. "Thank you for sharing that! It's so helpful."

As we turned to leave, I caught a glimpse of a nearby booth where a local journalist was setting up for an interview with the festival organizers. "Lila, let's see if he knows anything. Journalists often have a wealth of information."

We approached the journalist, who was arranging his notepad. "Hey there! Do you have a moment?" I asked.

"Sure, what's up?" he replied, looking up with interest.

"We're investigating any connection between Mayor Harrison and the murder victim. Do you know anything about their past dealings?" Lila jumped in.

"Ah, the mayor and the unfortunate victim. Quite the scandal, isn't it?" he said, tapping his pen against his notepad. "Harrison's past isn't as clean as it seems. He's had a few run-ins with the law before becoming mayor, but most people don't know the details."

"Like what?" I pressed, intrigued.

He hesitated for a moment, glancing around as if to ensure no one was listening. "There were rumors about him being involved in some shady business, but nothing ever stuck. It's hard to find concrete evidence in a small town like this."

I exchanged a glance with Lila, our thoughts aligning again. "What about the charity event?" I asked. "Did you ever hear any complaints about his involvement?"

"Oh, definitely. There were murmurs about funds going missing, but it was all swept under the rug," he said. "He's got a knack for making things disappear."

My mind raced as I processed this new information. "Do you think he had a motive to kill Ronald Waverly?"

"I wouldn't put it past him," the journalist replied, his expression serious. "Power can corrupt, and from the vibe I get from him, Harrison seems to be one who would do anything to keep his secrets buried."

Wow.

Chapter 12

BAD BUSINESS DEALS

I t wasn't long after we dug up the old dealings of Mayor Harrison that suspicions and rumors started to spread like wildfire. Whispers and side glances became the festival's soundtrack. The more we dug, the more questions we seemed to unearth. But answers? They were harder to come by.

Lila and I sat on the porch of Maplewood Haven, our eyes scanning the festival grounds in the distance. Mitz was curled up beside us, snoring softly as the cool autumn breeze rustled the leaves. The late morning sun cast a soft glow over everything, but I couldn't shake the cloud of uncertainty that hung above us.

"This whole thing is like a tangled web," Lila muttered, sipping her coffee. "Every time we think we're onto something, there seems to be another link to fit into the puzzle."

"Exactly. But the mayor isn't the only one acting strange."

Before Lila could respond, the sound of footsteps caught our attention. We both looked up to see Dennis heading towards us, his expression a mix of urgency and nerves.

"Morning, ladies," Dennis said, his voice tight as he approached. "I need to talk to you."

I shared a glance with Lila before nodding. "Sure, Dennis. What's on your mind?"

Dennis rubbed his hands together, clearly uncomfortable. He was a well-known face around town, always friendly and easygoing, but something about him felt off today. He shifted on his feet, his eyes darting around like he was afraid someone might overhear.

"It's about Edith," he said, lowering his voice.

Lila and I straightened in our seats. Edith had been on our radar for a while now, ever since we found out she had some sort of past connection with Ronald.

"What about Edith?" Lila asked, her eyes narrowing slightly.

Dennis glanced over his shoulder as if making sure no one else was around. "I think she's hiding something. Something important."

I crossed my arms, leaning forward. "Go on."

Dennis let out a heavy sigh, his eyes darting between us. "I've been hearing things—about her past, about her dealings with... well, certain people. I don't know all the details, but from what I've gathered, Edith had a falling out with Ronald years ago. Something big. And I'm starting to think she might be more involved in all of this than she's letting on."

Lila raised an eyebrow. "You're saying Edith might have had a motive?"

Dennis nodded quickly; his expression grim. "Exactly. And I don't think it's just a coincidence that she's been acting so strange lately. She's been avoiding people, keeping to herself more than usual. It's like she's trying to stay under the radar."

I exchanged a glance with Lila. Dennis didn't know what we already found out from Edith. He was throwing a lot of suspicion Edith's way, but something about his tone didn't sit right with me. It felt too deliberate, too calculated like he was trying to shift the focus away from himself.

"Why are you telling us this now, Dennis?" I asked, keeping my voice steady. "Why not go to the police?"

Dennis hesitated, rubbing the back of his neck. "Because I'm not sure if I'm right. I don't want to accuse her of something without proof. But you two... you might be able to put it together. I figured you might be able to figure out if there's something more to Edith's story."

Lila narrowed her eyes. "Or maybe you're trying to throw us off the scent. Make us look at Edith instead of you."

Dennis' eyes widened, and he shook his head vehemently. "No! That's not what I'm doing, I swear. I just... I don't want anyone else to get hurt."

I studied him for a moment, my gut telling me that Dennis wasn't being entirely truthful. But whether he was hiding something out of guilt or fear, I wasn't sure yet.

"We'll look into it," I said finally. "But if you're lying to us, Dennis—"

"I'm not," he interrupted, his voice pleading. "I'm telling you everything I know."

Lila and I didn't say anything else as Dennis turned and hurried away, leaving us more confused.

"Do you believe him?" Lila asked once he was out of earshot.

I sighed, leaning back in my chair. "I don't know. Something about the way he was acting feels off. Like he's trying too hard to pin this on Edith."

Lila nodded thoughtfully. "Yeah, but why? What's he so nervous about?"

"That's what we need to figure out." I stood, feeling the weight of the investigation pressing down on me. "Let's head into town. I have a feeling Edith might be able to shed some light on this."

***

We find Edith hanging out near the pumpkin carving tent. Putting together the last-minute details of the pumpkin carving contest.

"Hi, Edith," I call out.

"Molly, Lila!" she greeted us warmly. "Are you looking forward to the big contest?"

"Actually, we were hoping to talk to you," I said, keeping my tone light but purposeful. "About something that happened a long time ago."

Edith raised an eyebrow, wiping her hands on a towel. "Sounds serious."

"It is," Lila chimed in. "We need to know more about your connection to Ronald Waverly."

The smile on Edith's face faltered, and she suddenly acted a lot less cheerful. "I don't know what more I can tell you."

"We know he was blackmailing you all those years. But what about now, what more can you tell us about why he would have been here now during the festival." I urged gently. "We were told you know more about that."

Edith's expression shifted, her eyes narrowing slightly as she glanced between us. For a moment, she seemed to be debating whether to tell us anything. Then she sighed, running a hand through her hair.

"Ok," she said quietly. "I know he had a hand in many of the real estate deals in town."

Lila and I exchanged a glance, waiting for her to continue.

"Years ago," Edith began, her voice barely above a whisper, "He was involved in a real estate deal. He was an investor in several start-up businesses that came to Maple Lake. It was supposed to be a simple partnership—he'd help get them up and running, and in return, he wanted a percentage of the profits. But things went south. He wanted more than his fair share, and when they refused, he threatened to ruin them."

I felt a knot form in my stomach. "And did he?"

Edith shook her head, her eyes filled with regret. "No. From what I understand, one by one they all cut ties with him. But I always knew he held a grudge. He was the type of man who didn't forget, and he didn't forgive."

Lila frowned. "So, you think he came back to town to settle the score?"

"I don't know," Edith admitted. "But I wouldn't be surprised. He always said they'd regret crossing him."

"So, why didn't you come forward about this sooner?" I asked, my voice softening.

Edith looked down at her hands, guilt flashing across her face. "Because I was afraid. I didn't want to remind him he had grounds to ruin me as well."

Lila crossed her arms, her expression hard to read. "Dennis seems to think you know something more."

Edith's head snapped up; her eyes wide. "Dennis? Why would he say that?"

"That's what we were hoping you could tell us," I said.

Edith shook her head, her face pale. "I don't understand. Dennis had nothing to do with that."

"Edith," I said gently, "is there something else you're not telling us? Anything more regarding Dennis?"

I exchanged a glance with Lila, the pieces of the puzzle starting to come together. Dennis seemed to want to throw suspicion on Edith, so I couldn't help but wonder if they both knew more. The question was: what?

She hesitated, her eyes flickering with uncertainty. "I... I don't know."

"Whatever it is," Lila added, "it could help us figure out who's behind all of this."

Edith looked down at her hands, her voice barely a whisper. "Dennis and I... we've been working together. But it's not what you think. We've been trying to protect the town from people like him. People like Ronald Waverly."

My breath caught in my throat. "What do you mean?"

Edith met my gaze, her expression filled with regret. "There's more to this than just an old business deal. Ronald wasn't just here for revenge. He was involved in something much bigger—something that could destroy Maple Lake."

Chapter 13

MAN TO MAN

The cool evening air brushed against my skin as I walked beside Jake, the sun slowly dipping below the horizon. The festival had calmed down, and the crowd had thinned, leaving a more peaceful atmosphere. But inside, my nerves were anything but calm.

Jake's presence beside me was a steadying force, his quiet strength radiating. I had debated whether or not to tell Jake about all the pieces Lila and I had uncovered, especially after our encounter with Dennis and Edith. But now, after so many twists, I realized Jake needed to be in the loop.

"Max still hasn't been around much," I muttered, breaking the silence between us.

Jake gave a small nod, his jaw clenched like it always did when he was deep in thought. "He's definitely got something weighing on him. I feel bad for him."

"I know," I said, pushing back the doubts. "But he's been too evasive, Jake. It's like he's terrified of something coming to light. It might not be murder, but then we need to find out what it is."

"Maybe I should talk to him man to man," Jake suggested. "Maybe he'll open up."

"That's a great idea. I know Lila would love to have the old Max back."

"I'll stop by to see him, I promise." Jake squeezed my hand.

I filled Jake in on all the new leads Lila and I had dug up earlier—the real estate flyer and the information about Vincent Harrison's old dealings with the fundraiser and the missing funds. Even the comments from the journalist were disturbing.

Jake stopped, turning to face me. "Wow, that's a lot. No wonder you're so stressed."

Mitz trotted beside us, his tiny paws making soft taps against the pavement. He, at least, seemed blissfully unaware of the tension hanging in the air.

I exhaled slowly, my mind spinning as Jake walked me back to Maplewood Haven.

Jake nodded; his gaze distant. "I think we need to focus on the facts we have now. Mayor Harrison, Edith, Dennis... they're still on the table. Max not likely. I'll drop by his shop. He should be closing up by now. I'll see you tomorrow. Some rest will help clear your head." He placed a thoughtful peck on my forehead.

I couldn't argue with that. The puzzle pieces were all there, but they weren't fitting together yet. And the longer it took to solve this, the more dangerous it felt.

Mitz let out a small bark, and I looked down at him, smiling despite everything. At least one of us was still in good spirits.

***

Jake headed back toward town. He looked like a man on a mission as he disappeared toward Max's pet store. I sure hope he finds answers.

Jake knocked on the window of the pet store, and Max looked up from his work. "Hi Jake, you're here late. What's up?"

"I was hoping you might be willing to talk with me man to man. Molly and Lila are really worried about you. How are you doing?" Jake pried.

"I really am fine," Max assured him. "I know I seem on edge lately but trust me. You'll understand soon."

"What do you mean by that?" Jake pressed.

"I just need a bit more time. But it'll all be clear soon." Max's face was serious.

"Ok, Max." Jake reluctantly agreed. "But if you don't fix this soon, you're going to lose Lila."

"Soon, Jake, I promise," Max assured.

Chapter 14
SHADY DEALS

The crisp fall air stung my cheeks as I walked through Maplewood Haven's garden, trying to shake off the nagging frustration that had settled in since our investigation into Edith and Dennis had stalled. For the past couple days, Lila and I had been chasing down every lead involving them, but none of it was adding up.

Mitz ran ahead, chasing a stray leaf that danced in the breeze, his little legs moving quickly as if nothing in the world was wrong. I smiled at him, trying to take comfort in his simple joy, but the growing weight of the unsolved mystery pressed heavily on my shoulders.

Lila caught up with me, her face drawn in a frown. "I can't believe it's leading nowhere with Edith and Dennis. It feels like we're missing something, but I just don't know what it is. And on top of everything, I feel like I'm losing Max."

I nodded, my thoughts swirling. I felt bad for her. I know she thought Max was the one for her.

"Let's get this thing solved so we can get back to our lives."

Dennis had gone out of his way to cast suspicion on Edith, but after digging into their lives, nothing about either of them seemed to point to murder. Edith, while prickly and secretive, was too deeply entrenched in her small-town gossip circles to keep such a dark secret. Dennis, though cagey and secretive, wasn't the type to act out of malice. But whatever secrets they were guarding, it didn't seem to relate to the death.

"Chief Monroe still hasn't put anything together either," I muttered. "He said we need more substantial evidence if we're going to point any fingers."

Lila crossed her arms, shaking her head. "So where do we go from here? We're running in circles."

I glanced at her, feeling the same frustration gnawing at me. It was true—the dead ends with Edith and Dennis had left us grasping for something solid. But there was one name we kept coming back to, one that we had tried to push aside for too long.

"The mayor," I said, more to myself than to Lila.

Lila's brow furrowed. "But what's his motive. All we have is that he's into some real estate stuff and that he may have had some sticky fingers in the past... so what's his reason for murder?"

"I don't know," I replied slowly. "Something's still off about him. For a man who thrives on being in control of everything, he's been keeping his head down since the festival started. And that doesn't sit right with me."

Lila sighed, her gaze wandering to the autumn trees that lined the property. "He did have that old connection with Ronald... maybe we need to start digging into his past again. It feels like there's more to that story than what we've uncovered."

A chill ran down my spine as I thought about the mayor's polished exterior—the way he seemed to glide through town with his perfectly rehearsed smile and charm. But beneath the surface, there was something darker, something we hadn't yet identified.

"I'll start looking into old records," I said. "There has to be something there. No one rises to power in a small town like Maple Lake without leaving a trail."

Lila nodded. "Good idea. I'll keep asking around to see if anyone else has stories about Harrison. And then later, I'm going to see Max. I can't wait any more. I just need to know if we're over."

"Alright. Good luck with that." I gave her hand a squeeze of support.

We spent the rest of the afternoon following through on our plan. While Lila met with various townspeople who might have known Harrison before he became mayor, I went straight to the town archives. The dusty, dimly lit room in the town hall wasn't exactly welcoming, but it was exactly where I needed to be.

I pulled up old newspaper clippings, town meeting minutes...anything that might give me insight into Vincent's rise to power. It was slow going, and after hours of sorting through records, I was beginning to lose hope. But then, I found something—a small article, buried in a local paper from over a decade ago, caught my eye.

It wasn't about Mayor Harrison directly, but it mentioned his involvement in a business deal gone wrong. According to the article, he had backed a land development project that had fallen apart after accusations of fraud. The deal had been quietly swept under the rug, but the damage it did to those involved lingered for years.

I felt a twinge of excitement. This could be it—a hidden part of Harrison's past that had been carefully concealed.

I copied down the details, then hurried out of the archives to meet Lila.

We reconvened at The Maple Mug. The familiar aroma filled the air, offering a small sense of comfort amidst the chaos. Jake was there having his lunch. As I walked in, Jake raised an eyebrow, sensing I had something.

"What did you find?" he asked, patting the seat next to him.

I ordered a cup of coffee and took a sip, savoring the warmth before diving in. "There was a development project Vincent Harrison was involved in years ago. It collapsed under suspicious circumstances. Fraud accusations, though nothing was proven."

Lila's eyes widened. "That could be something. Maybe Ronald was involved somehow?"

"That's what I'm thinking," I said. "It wasn't mentioned directly in the article, but if the mayor had shady dealings back then, there's a good chance he's still hiding something."

Jake leaned against the counter; his face thoughtful. "We need to find out who else was involved in that deal. Someone out there might still hold a grudge."

I nodded, already thinking about our next move. "And we need to confront Mayor Harrison again. We can't tiptoe around him any longer. If he's hiding something, we need to push him."

"I've got to get back to the store, but I'll catch up with you two later. Be careful." Jake put a hand on my shoulder and headed out.

***

Lila and I headed to the town hall. The festival was still winding down, and the streets were relatively quiet, which gave us the perfect opportunity to catch the mayor off guard.

We were greeted by his secretary, who tried to wave us off, but I wasn't in the mood to be polite.

"We need to speak with the mayor," I said firmly. "Now."

The secretary blinked, clearly taken aback by the intensity in my voice. She hesitated, but before she could protest further, Harrison's voice rang out from his office.

"Let them in."

We exchanged a glance before walking into the mayor's office. Vincent sat behind his large mahogany desk, his posture as perfect as ever, though I noticed the slight flicker of discomfort in his eyes as we entered.

"Molly, Lila," he said, gesturing for us to sit. "To what do I owe the pleasure?"

I wasted no time. "We know about the land deal from ten years ago, Mayor. The one that collapsed under allegations of fraud. We know you were involved."

His face didn't change, but there was a momentary pause before he replied. "That was a long time ago. Nothing was ever proven, and it has nothing to do with what's happening now."

"Maybe not," I said, leaning forward in my chair, "but you've been acting suspicious ever since the murder. You've distanced yourself from the investigation, and you're not being forthcoming about things that could help solve this. You of all people should want this taken care of."

He leaned back, steepling his fingers. "You're making a lot of accusations, Molly, but I don't see any proof."

Lila, who had been silent until now, spoke up. "We're not here to throw accusations around, Mayor. We just want the truth. If you know something—anything—now's the time to come clean."

For the first time, Harrison's façade cracked. His eyes darkened, and his voice dropped. "You think you know me, don't you? You think I'm some kind of villain because I'm the mayor, and I've made deals that weren't always above board. But you don't understand what it takes to run this town. You don't know the pressures I deal with, the choices I've had to make."

I felt a chill run down my spine. There was something unhinged in his voice now, something desperate.

"I did what I had to do back then," Mayor Harrison continued, "to protect this town, to protect my future. And I'll do it again if I have to."

My heart raced. "What are you saying? Are you admitting to something?"

He smirked and his eyes narrowed. "I'm saying that sometimes, sacrifices have to be made for the greater good. And if you two keep digging where you shouldn't, you might find yourselves becoming the next sacrifice."

Lila gasped, and I clenched my fists, trying to keep my voice steady. "Is that a threat?"

Harrison stood, his towering figure casting a shadow over us. "Take it however you want. But if you want to keep your lives peaceful, I suggest you drop this and walk away. The past is buried for a reason."

His words hung heavily in the air, thick with menace, and for a moment, I could only stare at him, my heart pounding in my chest. The shift in the mayor's demeanor was undeniable, the polished politician giving way to something far darker and more calculating.

Lila and I stood in silence for a beat longer, then without another word, we turned and left his office. My mind raced as we walked down the long corridor of town hall, the sound of our footsteps echoing off the walls. I felt Lila's arm brush against mine, her tension matching my own.

We stepped outside, the crisp autumn air hitting our faces, but the coolness did nothing to ease the heat of fear that had settled in my gut.

"That was... intense," Lila finally said, her voice barely above a whisper.

I nodded, unable to shake the image of him towering over us, his eyes cold and unyielding. "He's hiding something big Lila. And he's willing to do whatever it takes to keep it hidden. He's involved. I no longer have any doubts."

"I got that feeling too," Lila agreed, glancing around nervously as if expecting someone to overhear us. "What now? Do we keep pushing, or do we take his warning seriously?"

I inhaled deeply, trying to calm my racing thoughts. "I think we need to regroup and figure out what our next move is. Harrison might have shown his hand, but that doesn't mean we can barge ahead without thinking. If he's desperate enough to threaten us, we need to be smart."

Lila nodded, her eyes hardening with determination. "We'll figure it out. We always do."

"I'm heading back to Maplewood Haven, are you coming?" My thoughts swirled with possibilities. Our mayor was clearly involved in something shady, but how deep did it go? And more importantly, how far was he willing to go to keep his secrets buried?

"No, I think I'll head over to see Max. I need to get this over with." Lila's frown spread across her face.

∗∗∗

By the time I reached the Haven, I had a plan forming in my head. We couldn't go straight back to Chief Monroe with just our suspicions—he needed proof. And if the mayor had anything to do with the murder, there had to be a trail, no matter how well he thought he'd covered his tracks.

Jake was waiting for me when I walked in, his face etched with concern. "You ok? You've been gone a while."

I offered him a small smile, trying to downplay the tension of the confrontation with Mayor Harrison. "I'm fine."

Jake raised an eyebrow but didn't push. "Well, I made dinner if you're hungry. Thought you might need a break."

"Thanks, Jake," I beamed gratefully. "You definitely know how to surprise me. I sure could use some food after the morning I've had."

I sat down in the kitchen for a few moments and allowed myself to relax, the warmth of this place always seems to provide a welcome reprieve from the chaos outside. Mitz, sensing my unease, jumped onto my lap and nuzzled into my side, his small body a comforting weight.

As we ate, Jake caught me up on the latest town gossip—most of it centered around the festival soon wrapping up and the usual small-town drama. But then he hesitated, and his gaze paused on me.

"There's something else I heard," he said slowly. "I wasn't sure if I should mention it, but… there's been more talk about Harrison. People are starting to wonder if he's involved in more than just town politics."

My fork froze halfway to my mouth. "What kind of talk?"

Jake glanced around as if checking to make sure no one was listening. "Some of the old-timers have been whispering about his past. I don't know all the details, but there's a rumor that he wasn't always so… polished. That he had some pretty shady dealings before he came to Maple Lake."

"Before Maple Lake?" My heart pounded. "That matches up with what we found," I said quietly. "That land deal years ago...fraud. I know he was involved, and it all just disappeared."

Jake frowned. "You think that's connected to the murder?"

"I'm starting to think so," I admitted, "especially after the way he reacted when we confronted him today."

Jake's eyes darkened. "What? Did he threaten you?"

"Not directly, but it was clear enough."

Jake clenched his jaw, anger flashing across his face. "That bastard. You need to be careful, Molly. Harrison's not the kind of man to take lightly."

"I know," I said softly, feeling the weight of his concern. "But we can't back down now. We're too close."

Jake was quiet for a moment, his gaze intense. "Just promise me you'll be careful. I don't like the idea of you getting mixed up in something dangerous."

I nodded, grateful for his concern. "I promise."

After dinner, we retreated to the parlor, determined to figure out our next move. We spread out the flyers and notes we'd gathered, going over everything again with fresh eyes. But the more we looked, the more it became clear that we were missing a critical piece of the puzzle.

"This all points to Harrison," I paced the room. "I can feel it, but I need more than just rumors and accusations. I need hard evidence."

Jake stopped my pacing and turned to me; his expression determined. "Then we need to find it. Let's go back through the town records, talk to more people, whatever it takes. We can't let him get away with this."

I agreed, but a part of me couldn't shake the lingering fear that we were walking into dangerous territory. Harrison had already shown that he was willing to threaten us to protect his secrets. What else was he capable of?

As I lay in bed late that night, staring at the ceiling, an idea struck me. Harrison wasn't just hiding something in his past—he was actively trying to cover it up. And if that was the case, there had to be someone else who knew the truth. Someone who had been involved in the land deal or had seen his dark side.

I sat up, my mind racing. We needed to find that person. The one who had been there when everything fell apart. The one who could expose him for who he really was.

I grabbed my phone and texted Lila: ***Tomorrow, we find the missing piece. Vincent's past is the key, and someone out there knows the truth. We just have to find them.***

Lila's response came almost immediately: ***Let's do it.***

With that, I lay back down, my mind buzzing with possibilities. Tomorrow, we would dig deeper than ever before. And this time, we wouldn't stop until we had the answers we needed.

Chapter 15

DEEP DIVE

T he next morning, Lila arrived earlier than ever. I sat in the parlor staring at the flyers and notes scattered before us. Mitz was curled up on the floor by the fireplace, occasionally glancing at us, sensing the tension hanging in the air.

I tapped my fingers against my mug, feeling a mix of frustration and determination. "Wow, you're early. How did it go with Max last night?"

"Well, we didn't get a chance to chat. When I got to the store, he was locking up early...so weird. I told him we needed to talk but he was in a crazy hurry. He asked if I'd go to the festival with him tomorrow for the final day. I don't know Molly. He's all over the place. I don't know what to do about us anymore." Lila said yawning. "That's why I saw your text so late. I haven't slept.

Shaking my head I just looked at her. "I guess that's our next mystery."

"So where did you end up with things last night?" Lila changed the subject.

"We've been going in circles, Lila. We both know that. But last night I realized that the mayor's still involved, or he wouldn't have reacted like that. These dealings had to include other players. That's who we need to find. There has to be someone who knows what he's hiding."

"That makes sense I guess." Lila looked like she needed the entire pot of coffee.

My thoughts wandered back to our conversation with Harrison the day before. His cold demeanor, the way he had threatened us, and the fact that he was so adamant about keeping his past buried. That was the key—his past. But not just any part of it—the parts that involved Ronald Waverly.

"We need to check into Ronald's history, not just the mayors," I said suddenly, sitting up straighter. "If they were connected before, there has to be some record of it. Maybe it wasn't public knowledge, but that doesn't mean it didn't happen."

Lila's eyes lit up with understanding. "That's it! We've been focusing so much on Harrison that we forgot to dig deeper into Ronald. If they were in business together or had a falling out, we might find something in Ronald's background."

I nodded, my heart racing as the pieces began to click into place. "We need to go back to the town hall. There might be records of Ronald's past dealings there—business records, financial statements, anything that links him to Harrison."

Lila agreed, and we quickly gathered our things, determined to chase down this new lead. The walk to town hall was brisk, the autumn wind biting at our cheeks, but I barely felt the chill. My mind was too focused on what we might uncover.

When we arrived at town hall, the receptionist gave us a curious look as we signed in, but I didn't care. We weren't here for small talk. We were here for answers.

We headed straight to the records room, where the clerk, Mrs. Harper, greeted us with a polite smile. "Back again, ladies? You two sure have been spending a lot of time digging through old files lately."

"We're trying to help Chief Monroe with the investigation," I explained, keeping my tone casual. "There's still a lot we don't know about the victim."

Mrs. Harper raised an eyebrow. "Well, I hope you find what you're looking for. You know where everything is, so feel free to take your time."

With that, she returned to her desk, and Lila and I set to work. We knew this wasn't going to be easy. Town records could be extensive, and we weren't sure where to start. But if there was something in Ronald Waverly's past that connected him to Mayor Harrison, we were going to find it.

We divided up the workload, Lila taking the financial records while I focused on the business dealings. Hours passed as we sifted through file after file, the clock ticking in the background. My eyes began to blur from the endless pages, but I kept going, determined not to miss a single detail.

It wasn't until I was halfway through a stack of business contracts from years ago that something caught my eye—a familiar name, buried in the fine print of a land development deal. I froze, my heart skipping a beat.

"Lila," I whispered, my voice barely audible as I stared at the document in my hands.

Lila peaked up from her stack of papers. "What is it?"

I gave her the document, my hands trembling. "Look at this. Ronald was involved in that land development deal... with Harrison."

Lila's eyes widened as she scanned the page. "Oh my... This is it. This is what we've been searching for."

I nodded, my pulse racing. The deal was from years ago, long before Harrison had become mayor. It was a large project, one that had promised big returns for everyone involved. But the deal had fallen apart under mysterious circumstances, and Ronald had walked away with nothing. Harrison, on the other hand, had somehow managed to come out on top, despite the project's failure.

"This explains so much," Lila said, her voice barely above a whisper. "Ronald must have been holding a grudge against Harrison for years. He probably blamed him for the deal falling apart."

"And Harrison has been trying to bury this ever since," I added, my mind racing as I pieced it all together. "Ronald must have come back to Maple Lake recently, maybe to confront him about what happened. That's why Harrison has been acting so strange—he knew Ronald could expose his past."

Lila shook her head in disbelief. "But why murder? How could he go that far?"

I stared at the document in my hands, the weight of it heavy in my chest. "Because if Ronald had proof of Harrison's involvement in the failed deal, one he benefitted from while it ruined everyone else. That could ruin him. Not just as mayor, but his entire reputation. He could lose everything."

Lila's face hardened. "And that's exactly what Ronald must have threatened to do. He probably came here wanting revenge, and Harrison panicked."

It all made sense now. The mayor had been trying to protect his secrets, but Ronald's arrival had thrown everything into chaos. He couldn't risk his past coming to light, so he had resorted to the unthinkable—murder.

"We need to get this to Chief Monroe," I said, my voice firm. "This is the missing piece. This is the proof we've been looking for."

Lila nodded, already gathering the rest of the papers. "Let's go."

We hurried out of the records room, our hearts pounding with urgency. As we made our way to the police station, I couldn't shake the feeling that we were right on top of the truth, but at the same time, I knew we were walking into dangerous territory. Harrison wasn't going to let this go easily. He had already shown that he was willing to threaten us, and now that we had proof of his involvement, I couldn't help but wonder what he would do next.

When we arrived at the station, Chief Monroe greeted us with a curious look. "What brings you two here?"

"We found something," I said, handing him the document. "This ties Ronald to Mayor Harrison. They were involved in a shady land deal years ago. Ronald lost everything, but Harrison somehow came out like a bandit."

Chief Monroe's eyes darkened as he read through the document. "This is big," he muttered under his breath. "If this is true, it gives Harrison a strong motive for the murder."

"Exactly," Lila added. "Ronald must have come back to town to confront him, and Harrison panicked. He didn't want his past to be exposed."

Chief Monroe looked up at us, his expression serious. "This changes everything. I'll need to look into this further, but you two might have just cracked this case wide open."

A sense of relief washed over me, but it was quickly tempered by the realization that we weren't out of the woods yet. Now that we had gone to the chief with proof of Harrison's involvement, we were in more danger than ever.

Chapter 16

THE CONFRONTATION

The Maple Lake Fall Festival was in full swing by the time I arrived. The air was filled with the smell of roasted chestnuts and the sound of children laughing as they ran between the colorful stalls. But despite the festive atmosphere, my mind was far from light-hearted. Lila and I had discovered the connection between Harrison and Ronald Waverly—a shady business deal that had gone sour. It gave the mayor motive. I knew Harrison wasn't going to give up easily.

Jake met me by the entrance, his expression as serious as mine. "He's here," Jake said, nodding toward the large pavilion where the mayor was shaking hands and making small talk with the townsfolk. "He's been acting off all morning."

I followed Jake's gaze, watching as Harrison plastered a tight, forced smile on his face while talking to a group of elderly ladies. Even from a distance, I could see the nervous energy radiating off him. His hands fidgeted at his sides, and his eyes kept darting around the festival grounds as if he were expecting someone to jump out from behind the tents and confront him.

"Do you think he knows we've got something on him?" I asked Jake quietly, though the answer seemed obvious. "It looks like his paranoia's getting to him."

"I think he's scared," Jake replied. "And scared men make mistakes. We need to push him, Molly."

I nodded, my heart pounding with both anxiety and determination. "Let's do it."

Together, Jake and I made our way through the bustling crowd toward the pavilion where the mayor stood. He saw us coming and his expression faltered for just a second before he quickly composed himself. But that moment of fear in his eyes didn't go unnoticed.

"Molly, Jake," Mayor Harrison greeted us with a strained smile. "Enjoying the festival?"

"We were," Jake said, his tone casual but with an edge to it. "But we were hoping to have a word with you, Mayor. In private."

Harrison hesitated, glancing around at the festivalgoers as if trying to calculate his next move. "I'm rather busy at the moment," he said, his voice a bit too cheerful. "Perhaps later?"

"This won't take long," I added, stepping closer. "It's about your past dealings with Ronald Waverly. You remember him, don't you?"

His smile faltered again, but he quickly recovered, straightening his jacket as if that could shield him from the weight of our questions. "I don't know what you're talking about," Harrison replied, but his voice wavered slightly, betraying the calm demeanor he was trying to project. "I had no dealings with that man. I've already told the police everything I know."

"You didn't tell them everything," Jake said, crossing his arms. "Like the fact that you and Ronald were involved in a land development deal years ago. The one that went belly-up. You walked away with your reputation intact and your pockets full, but he didn't."

Harrison's face paled, and for a moment, I thought he might crack then and there. But instead, he straightened his back and shot us both a stern look. "That's ridiculous. I have no idea what you're talking about. Whatever records you've dug up are irrelevant to this investigation."

"They're not irrelevant when they give you a motive," I countered, my voice firmer than before. "Ronald came back to town to confront you, didn't he? He wanted revenge for what happened with the deal."

The mayor's jaw clenched, his eyes narrowing. "You're making wild accusations without a shred of proof."

"We have the documents, Mayor," Jake said, his voice low and intense. "We know about the deal. We know what happened."

For a long moment, Harrison didn't say anything. He just stood there, staring at us, his chest rising and falling in shallow breaths. The sounds of the festival seemed distant, muffled by the tension between us. I could almost hear the gears turning in his mind as he tried to figure out his next move.

Finally, he let out a slow breath, running a hand through his thinning hair. "That deal was years ago," he said, his voice quiet but strained. "I had no idea it would come back to haunt me like this. But I didn't kill him."

"Then what are you so nervous about?" Jake pressed. "If you're innocent, why dodge our questions? Why act like you've got something to hide?"

Harrison's eyes darted to the crowd again, as if looking for an escape. "This isn't a conversation we should be having here," he muttered. "People are watching."

"People are always watching, Mayor," I said, crossing my arms and standing my ground. "That's part of being the mayor, isn't it? You're used to the spotlight. So why is this making you sweat?"

Harrison's face flushed a deeper shade of red, his hands clenching into fists at his sides. "I told you; I didn't kill him! Yes, we had a deal that went wrong, but that was years ago. I've moved on. He hadn't, apparently, but that's not my fault."

"So, what did happen when he came back to town?" I asked, my voice softer now, trying to draw him out. "What did he want from you, Mayor? Did he threaten you?"

Harrison hesitated, glancing around nervously again before finally lowering his voice. "He...he showed up out of the blue," he admitted. "Said he wanted compensation for what he lost. Said he'd expose everything if I didn't pay up. It was blackmail."

I exchanged a glance with Jake. Blackmail. That was a serious accusation, and it added another layer to Ronald Waverly's motives for being in town. But it still didn't explain why the mayor was so rattled. Blackmail didn't necessarily lead to murder—unless the blackmailer pushed too far.

"Did you agree to pay him?" Jake asked, his voice steady.

Harrison shook his head. "Of course not. I told him to get lost, that I wasn't going to let him ruin me over something that was ancient history. I thought that was the end of it."

"But it wasn't," I said quietly. "He kept pushing, didn't he?"

The mayor's jaw tightened, and for a moment, I thought he might refuse to answer. But then he sighed, his shoulders sagging under the weight of his secret. "Yes," he admitted. "He came to my office the day before he was killed. He said if I didn't pay up, he'd go public with everything. He had records documenting the deal. I don't know how he got them, but they were damning."

"What did you do?" Jake asked, his eyes narrowing.

"I told him to leave," Harrison replied, his voice growing more agitated. "I told him he wasn't going to get a dime from me, and if he tried to blackmail me again, I'd have him arrested. He stormed out, and that was the last I saw of him."

"And the next day, he was dead," I said, my mind racing as the pieces of the puzzle started to come together.

Harrison's face grew more pale, his eyes darted nervously between us. "You can't seriously think I killed him," he said, his voice barely above a whisper. "I didn't. I swear. Yes, I was angry. Yes, I wanted him gone. But I didn't kill him. I would never—"

"We don't know what to think, Mayor," Jake interrupted, his voice cold. "You've been hiding things from the start, acting suspicious. You've given us every reason to believe you're involved."

Harrison swallowed hard, sweat beading on his forehead. "I didn't kill him," he repeated, his voice trembling. "You have to believe me."

I watched him closely, trying to gauge whether he was telling the truth. He appeared scared—terrified, even—but was it the fear of being wrongly accused, or the fear of getting caught?

Before I could say anything else, Mitz tugged at the leash, barking suddenly. I glanced down at him, surprised by the outburst. He was usually so calm during these tense moments as if sensing when to stay quiet. But now, his little body was stiff, his eyes fixed on something behind us.

I turned around to see Chief Monroe approaching us, his expression as grim as ever. He gave a nod to Jake and me before focusing on Harrison. "Mayor," he said in his usual low, gravelly tone. "We need to talk."

The mayor's face drained of color, and for a moment, I thought he might bolt. But he stayed rooted to the spot, his gaze flickering nervously between us and the chief.

"What is it, Chief?" I asked, sensing that something big was about to drop.

"Mayor," Chief Monroe said, stepping forward, "we're going to need you to come down to the station for questioning."

Harrison's eyes filled with desperation, and for a moment, I almost felt sorry for him. But then I remembered Ronald—the man who had been blackmailing him, who had turned up dead. The man who had been trying to expose his secrets.

And now, it seemed, those secrets were finally catching up to him.

"Fine," Harrison muttered, his shoulders slumping in defeat. "I'll come. But I didn't kill him. I swear on my life that I didn't kill him."

He turned to Chief Monroe and smirked.

"Just questioning, right?"

Chapter 17

LILA AND MAX

Lila arrived at Max's pet store a bit apprehensive. Finally, she could have Max's attention to herself. "Good morning, Max. Are you ready to go?"

Max seemed to fumble around a bit longer, then walked toward Lila. "Yes, as ready as I can be...ah yes, let's go."

"It seemed like we missed the majority of the festival. I'm so glad we are able to go together today, Max." Lila forced a smile and looked up at Max.

As they walked into the festival, the scent of apple cider filled the air. People were scattered everywhere, laughing and enjoying the festivities, thoughts of the tragedy now a distant memory.

We move through the crowds and stopped for a piece of freshly baked apple pie. But something was still off with Max. He went through all the actions, but Lila became more tense as the minutes passed.

"Max, I can't do this...we need to have a talk." Lila blurted out as if exhaling fiercely.

Max was caught off guard, seemingly stunned, "I know Lila. I'm sorry I've been so strange lately. Come with me." He pulled Lila's arm, leading her out of the crowd and closer to the pumpkin carving tent. He seemed adamant this is where we should talk.

"Please tell me what's wrong, Max. I can't take it anymore. Did I do something? I feel like you've been avoiding me all week. I refuse to believe you had anything to do with the murder, so what's going on in your head. I know it's not all this investigation chaos." Lila spiraled.

Max interrupted grabbing Lila's hand. "Oh my...I never meant to make you feel like you did anything wrong. Lila, you've been nothing but wonderful to me since we met. I don't think I would have made it through everything if it weren't for you. You mean the world to me."

"Then why?" Lila continued. "What happened to us? I feel the same way, but then it was like you forgot I existed."

"No, no." Max chuckled. Lila looked perturbed. "Lila, it's just the opposite. You've been nothing but on my mind. In fact, to hear you say that makes this so much easier. I was afraid I might have been reading you wrong."

Lila was totally confused now, evident by the twisted expression on her face. "I don't find this funny, Max."

"Lila, you might change your mind. I mean, wow, let me continue." Max faced Lila and gazed intently into her eyes.

"My life before Maple Lake was a disaster. I never could have dreamed that I would dig myself out of that. If it weren't for you and Molly getting all tangled up in my mess, well, let's just say that I may not be here today. I owe you my life, Lila. Then you stood by me while I was getting back on my feet. You have no idea how much I waited for your visits at the hospital. You are like a ray of sunshine. You brighten every room you step into. My life now feels like something I never thought I deserved, and it's all thanks to you. My store's doing great. I love Maple Lake and... Well, Lila, I love you."

Lila's face heated up and her cheeks blushed. "Wow, Max, I was not expecting that."

"Lila, there's more. So much more. I can't imagine ever being without you. I planned to surprise you at this year's festival when they announce the pumpkin contest winner. But that all got ruined with this murder chaos, and I've been scrambling to figure it out and...so, well, here it goes...Lila Montgomery, would you complete my wildest dreams and be my wife?" Max fumbled nervously and reached into his pocket. Kneeling in front of me, he held out the most sparkling diamond I'd ever imagined.

"Oh, my goodness!" Lila squealed. "Absolutely, I would love to be your wife, Max. I love you so much."

Max's arms never felt so good wrapped tightly around me. "Let's go find the others. We have some celebrating to do."

Hand in hand we headed to find Molly and Jake. As we strolled through the crowd, I filled Max in about the threats Molly and I got from Mayor Harrison when we questioned his involvement.

Max was furious. "Are you kidding me? In that case, the celebrating may have to wait a bit, Lila. I won't have anyone threatening my fiancée. We need to finish this thing."

Chapter 18

RANDALL

C hief Monroe had always been the calm, collected type, but to-day, frustration radiated off him in waves. His normally sharp eyes were tired, and he ran a hand over his face as if that would clear the haze of confusion surrounding the case.

"I don't get it," he muttered, pacing in his office. "There is nothing that ties Harrison directly to the murder. No prints, no weapon, only a potential motive. Dang it."

I exchanged a glance with Jake, who sat beside me with his arms crossed. His usual confident demeanor hid any trace of worry. Lila and Max arrived too, standing awkwardly by the door, silent witnesses to Chief Monroe's outburst. I could see the tension in their eyes, too. We were all feeling it—the frustration of coming so close and yet being stonewalled by the mayor's slippery ways.

"I still don't trust him," Jake said, his voice low but firm. "He was nervous during that last conversation. He's involved. I know it."

Chief Monroe stopped pacing and turned to face us, his expression hard. "I can't hold someone on a hunch, Jake. He's free until we find something concrete. I can't act without proof, no matter how much I think you're right."

Chief's words only fueled the frustration bubbling up in me. After all the clues we'd uncovered about Mayor Harrison's shady dealings with Ronald Waverly, it felt like the truth was right there, just out of reach. But nothing solid, no smoking gun to tie the mayor to the crime. My stomach knotted with the unfairness of it all.

"We're wasting time," Lila said, her voice sharp. She glanced over at me, her eyes blazing with determination. "If Chief Monroe's hands are tied, we need to dig deeper. There's got to be something else in Harrison's history that can help us."

Max, who had been unusually quiet, nodded in agreement. "He's hiding something, I know it. I've seen men like him before—always covering their tracks until it's too late."

I raised an eyebrow at Max, surprised. His past did give him some insight into people with ill intentions, but now it suddenly felt like he was stepping up. "You're probably right, Max," I said. "I agree. We're running out of time, and we need to find something solid soon."

Chief Monroe let out a heavy sigh, clearly frustrated that he couldn't push the case further for now. "I'll keep my eyes on him. Do what you need to. Just be careful—don't get yourselves in too deep."

Jake stood up, and his posture alone told me he was ready to act. He looked at me, then at Lila and Max. "Let's do this. We're not waiting for him to make another move."

We left the police station in silence, but once outside, I couldn't help but blurt out, "I feel like we're running around in circles." Mitz trotted along beside me, his little legs working hard to keep up. Even he seemed on edge, sensing the tension.

Jake let out a slow breath and put a hand on my shoulder. "We'll find something. I'm sure of it."

"I'm trying to wrap my head around everything we know. What's our next step?" I asked, looking from Jake to Lila to Max.

Lila stopped pacing and faced me. "There must be more in his past that we don't know. We've uncovered some of his shady business dealings with Ronald, but nothing concrete enough to prove his involvement."

"I bet if we look into his old business records or maybe speak to some of his old associates, we'll find something," Max said quietly, though his voice held a note of confidence I wasn't used to hearing from him.

Jake nodded. "We need to check into every deal he's made, every shady transaction. Someone has to know something. He can't hide it all."

I smiled at Jake, a surge of warmth flooding me despite the situation. He was right. We had to be relentless if we wanted to get anywhere. "Let's start by checking any old records we can get our hands on. And maybe a visit to a few people he used to do business with wouldn't hurt."

Lila looked energized by the plan. "Agreed. We should split up—some of us can start digging into records, and the rest of us can ask around town."

Max, surprisingly eager, chimed in. "I'll head to the local archives. I know my way around business records."

Jake raised an eyebrow but didn't say anything, instead giving a quick nod of approval. "Molly and I can go back to a few of Harrison's former business partners. They might have some useful information."

Lila smiled, looking hopeful. "And I'll see if there's anyone else in town who might know something. The mayor isn't exactly shy about flaunting his power."

We quickly split off, each of us determined to pull our weight in uncovering the truth. There was no time to waste. Zipping my coat up tighter, Jake and I started heading toward the edge of town when Mitz suddenly jumped up, his eyes wide and his tail wagging.

"Looks like someone else is determined to be in on the action," I chuckled, bending down to scratch his ears. "Of course boy, you're coming with us."

Jake grinned, grabbing a treat from his pocket. "I think he's our good luck charm. Besides, maybe he'll sniff something out we can't."

With Mitz in tow, we headed toward the part of town where Harrison's real estate associate lived, he was listed on the flyer along with the mayor, so we were hopeful he'd have some information. The cold autumn breeze nipped at my cheeks as we walked, the golden leaves rustling underfoot. Jake's pace was brisk, his usual laid-back demeanor replaced by the tension of the situation.

"Molly," Jake started, his voice thoughtful, "what do you think? I mean really think. Do you believe Harrison's capable of this?"

I sighed, looking ahead at the narrow street lined with old homes. "I don't know, Jake. I've always known him as the mayor with the perfect public image—everyone in town respects him. But the more we dig, the more I'm starting to see cracks in that persona. I'm starting to believe he's more corrupt than that three-piece suit let's on."

Jake nodded, deep in thought. "Yeah, the cracks are showing. But what kind of man hides this well for so long?"

We arrived at the house of his partner, Mr. Randall Evans, a former contractor who had been involved in some real estate deals back in the day. His house was a modest, weathered building that looked like it hadn't been touched in years. As we knocked on the door, I felt a familiar prickle of nerves, the weight of the investigation pressing on me.

Randall answered, his bushy gray eyebrows shooting up when he saw us standing there with Mitz. "Can I help you?" His voice was gruff, and I could tell he wasn't too thrilled about visitors.

"We were hoping to ask you a few questions about your past business with Mayor Harrison," I said, trying to keep my tone polite but firm. Mitz let out a small yip, almost as if he were encouraging me.

Randall frowned. "Vincent? What's this about? That was a long time ago. I don't deal with him anymore."

Jake stepped in, his authoritative presence making Randall shift uncomfortably. "We know you don't, but it's important that we understand more about that piece of history—things that might have happened behind the scenes. We believe the mayor is involved in something serious, and we're running out of time."

Randall's face twitched, a brief flicker of something passing through his eyes. He looked down at Mitz, who was staring up at him with unblinking eyes. Finally, Randall sighed. "Fine, come in."

The inside of his house was as run-down as the outside. Dust coated the furniture, and the place had the smell of stale tobacco. He gestured for us to sit on the worn-out couch as he lowered himself into a creaky armchair.

"Look," Randall began, lighting up a cigarette, "Vincent was always the type to play things close to the chest. We did business together, yeah, but there was always something sketchy about him. The man had connections—money would change hands, and paperwork would disappear. I'm guessing you already knew that, though."

I leaned forward, feeling the excitement in my chest grow. "Do you remember any specific deals? Something that might connect him to the victim from the festival?"

Randall took a long drag from his cigarette, exhaling slowly before answering. "There was one deal, about five years ago. Vincent wanted to invest in this development project outside of town—some new land that was supposed to be turned into luxury vacation homes. It all fell apart when his partner pulled out at the last minute. That partner was Ronald Waverly."

Jake's eyes narrowed. "And why did he pull out?"

Randall shrugged. "Couldn't say for sure, but rumor had it, he found out Vincent had been funneling money into something illegal. He got cold feet and backed out before the project could get off the ground. Vincent was livid."

I exchanged a glance with Jake. This was the first solid connection we'd found. Vincent had a clear motive—anger and betrayal.

Randall snubbed out his cigarette and leaned forward, his voice lowering to a near whisper. "If you ask me, that's when Vincent started spiraling. He's got secrets, deep ones."

Just as Randall was about to continue, the door behind him creaked open. I turned to see a tall figure standing in the doorway, shadowed by the dim light.

"Randall," the figure called sternly. "We need to go. Now."

Randall stiffened and quickly shut his mouth, his face paling as he glanced back at us.

"I can't say anymore. I've already said too much," he muttered hurriedly, stepping away.

Before either of us could respond, Randall turned and followed the figure out of the room, leaving us standing in silence, questions still swirling in our minds.

Chapter 19

MITZ'S FINDS

The late afternoon sun cast long shadows over Maple Lake as Lila, Jake, and I huddled near the corner of the festival grounds. Mitz trotted ahead, his nose to the ground, sniffing away like a detective on a mission. Since Randall's abrupt departure, we had been at a standstill, unsure of where to go next. Chief Monroe's frustration with the investigation wasn't helping matters either. We were running out of time, and everyone in town could feel the tension thickening with each passing hour.

Mitz barked suddenly, jolting me out of my thoughts. He circled a spot near the festival stage, paws scrabbling at the dirt.

"What's he got now?" Lila asked, hurrying over. Jake and I followed close behind. Mitz had never been one to bark without reason.

I knelt beside him, brushing away the loose dirt. At first, it looked like nothing—a few scattered leaves, and some festival debris—but then something glinted in the fading light.

"Wait, what's that?" I muttered, digging deeper. My fingers closed around something smooth and cold. I lifted it carefully from the dirt.

It was a pocket watch—old and worn, but unmistakably familiar. My heart skipped a beat as I turned it over in my hands, inspecting the intricate engravings on its surface. The faint outline of initials caught my eye: ***V.H.***

"Vincent Harrison," Jake breathed, leaning in closer.

Lila gasped softly. "You don't think..."

I stood up, my heart pounding as I stared at the bloodstain smeared across the edge of the watch. "This belonged to the mayor," I whispered, the realization sinking in. "He was wearing it the night of his speech."

Jake nodded. "Yes, I remember seeing it on him. He always had that watch on. His 'pride and joy,' he called it."

The three of us stood in stunned silence for a moment, the weight of the discovery pressing down on us. The blood on the watch couldn't be ignored. It was undeniable proof that Mayor Harrison had been involved.

Lila broke the silence, her voice barely above a whisper. "But why would he lose it here? Was this the scene of the murder... what does it mean for everything else we've found?"

As if on cue, Mitz barked again. This time, he nosed further under the stage, pushing through the draped curtain. Just below the podium, he pulled out something else. I rushed to him, my breath catching in my throat as I saw it...

A bloodied white glove. My blood ran cold.

"Oh, my...," I gasped, staring at the objects. The bloodstained watch glistened in the fading light, catching us all off guard. "This is... this is it. This is our link."

Jake's eyes widened. "This watch puts him at the scene."

I nodded, still reeling. "It makes sense now. The knife we found earlier... it explains why there were no prints."

Lila covered her mouth, shaking her head. "I can't believe it. The mayor?"

"We have to take this to Chief Monroe," Jake said, his voice urgent. "This is the evidence we've been looking for."

But something didn't sit right with me. The bloodstained watch and the hidden glove—I couldn't shake the feeling that there was more to this than what we were seeing.

"Let's think about this for a second," I said, holding up the watch. "If Harrison's been so careful all this time, why would he leave this behind? Why didn't he cover his tracks better?"

"Maybe he didn't think anyone would find it," Jake offered.

"Or maybe he panicked," Lila added. "After the murder, everything happened so fast. He probably didn't have time to go back and retrieve it."

I wanted to believe that, but something still gnawed at me. The mayor was a lot of things, but careless wasn't one of them.

Before we could think it over further, the sound of approaching footsteps startled us. A small crowd had gathered at the far end of the festival grounds, their murmurs growing louder as they spotted us. Word had spread about the mayor, and people were starting to put the pieces together on their own.

"Is it true?" one woman called out.

"Is the mayor really involved?" another voice asked, panic creeping into their tone.

Jake stepped forward, holding his hands up in an attempt to calm the crowd. "Everyone, please, we're still looking into things. We don't have all the answers yet."

The crowd, however, wasn't easily placated. Rumors had been swirling around for days, and it seemed like the townspeople were at their breaking point. The tension in the air was palpable, and I could feel the weight of their expectations settling heavily on us.

Mitz, sensing the unease, moved closer to me, his small form pressed against my leg for comfort. I absentmindedly scratched behind his ears as I turned the bloodstained watch over in my hands again. This was damning evidence, no doubt. But how would we explain it to Chief Monroe without creating a frenzy?

Lila stepped forward; her voice steady but firm. "We can't jump to conclusions just yet. Yes, we've found some things that raise questions, but we still need to piece everything together."

The crowd grumbled, but they seemed to calm down—at least for the moment. Jake shot me a look, clearly worried. We were standing on a powder keg, and one wrong move could set the whole thing off.

I turned to him, lowering my voice so the crowd wouldn't hear. "We need to get this to Chief Monroe. Quietly."

Jake nodded, understanding immediately. "Let's move before things get out of hand."

We carefully tucked the watch away, and with a final reassuring wave to the townspeople, we slipped away from the festival grounds. As we walked, the weight of what we had just uncovered hung between us like a dark cloud.

"We're so close now," Lila murmured, her eyes reflecting a mixture of relief and unease. "But what if this isn't enough? What if he finds a way to weasel out of it?"

I didn't have an answer for her. The mayor was a slippery man, and even with all the evidence we'd uncovered, I couldn't shake the feeling that he still had a card up his sleeve.

When we finally reached Chief Monroe's office, I handed him the watch and glove, explaining how we'd found it and what we suspected. His eyes narrowed as he examined the pieces, his lips pressing into a thin line.

"This is enough to bring him in," he said at last, his voice low. "But you're right—Harrison's a cunning man. He won't go down without a fight."

"But the townspeople are already starting to turn on him," Jake said. "They're suspicious, and it won't take much to sway them completely."

Chief Monroe nodded; his expression grim. "Let's see how this plays out. But be careful—all of you. If the mayor is involved in this, he won't hesitate to protect himself, no matter the cost."

With that, we left the office, the gravity of our situation sinking in. We were standing on the edge of something dangerous, and we couldn't afford to misstep now.

As we walked back toward the center of town, I couldn't help but glance over my shoulder, a shiver running down my spine. The mayor had been playing a dangerous game, and now it was our turn to make the next move.

But with Mayor Harrison's smooth denial and the mounting pressure from the townspeople, one thing was becoming clear—this was far from over.

Chapter 20
THE ARREST

I stood outside the sheriff's office, the early morning sun casting long shadows across the pavement. The weight of the last few days pressed heavily on my shoulders. After countless twists and turns in this investigation, we had finally gathered enough evidence to confront Mayor Harrison directly. The excitement that buzzed through me was mingled with anxiety; we were nearing the climax of a storm I had never anticipated when I first arrived in Maple Lake.

I took a deep breath, clutching Mitz tightly in my arms. The little chihuahua had been my steadfast companion through this chaos, sensing my tension and responding with an unwavering loyalty that grounded me. He squirmed slightly as if sensing the urgency of the moment.

"Are you ready for this?" Jake asked, standing beside me, his expression serious yet hopeful.

"I think so," I replied, glancing at him. "But I can't shake the feeling that Harrison is going to try to talk his way out of this."

"He's good at that," Jake admitted, running a hand through his hair. "But we have to stay focused. If we catch him off guard, we might just get him to crack."

I nodded, swallowing hard as we stepped through the sheriff's office doors. The atmosphere inside was tense but charged with a sense of purpose. Chief Monroe was behind his desk, flipping through some papers, his brow furrowed in concentration. The moment he saw us, he leaned back in his chair, a determined look crossing his face.

"I've got everything I need to bring him in," Chief Monroe said, his voice low but firm. "Thanks to you all, especially that watch you found."

I could hardly believe we had gotten this far. "What do we know about Harrison's past?" I asked, eager to piece together the whole story before the confrontation.

Monroe shook his head, clearly frustrated. "He's always managed to keep things quiet. But there are whispers—rumors of shady deals, of involvement in land scams before he came here. His track record is... questionable at best."

The thought of a mayor hiding such a sordid past while serving the town was infuriating. I felt a surge of determination as I thought about all the townspeople who had trusted him, believing he was looking out for their best interests.

"Let's do this," Jake said, a steely glint in his eyes. "We can't let him keep lying to everyone."

With that, Chief Monroe picked up his phone and called for back-up. As he relayed the address, I felt a mix of anxiety and anticipation swirl within me. This was the moment we had worked toward, but I still feared how it would unfold.

Moments later, we were heading toward Harrison's office. The closer we got, the more my heart raced. I had seen how a web of deceit could unravel lives, and I desperately hoped that bringing him to justice would somehow restore faith in our community.

When we arrived at the mayor's office, Chief Monroe motioned for us to stay back while he and his deputies approached the door. I watched from a distance, my heart thudding in my chest as they knocked. Harrison's familiar figure appeared in the window, looking every bit the confident politician. But I knew the truth—he was anything but.

"Mayor Harrison!" Monroe called; his voice authoritative. "We have some questions for you. Open the door."

Harrison's expression shifted from surprise to irritation, but he opened the door, feigning a smile. "Chief Monroe, what's this about?"

"Mind if we come in?" Monroe asked, stepping inside.

The other deputies followed, and I could barely see the mayor's face twist into confusion as he glanced around, taking in the unexpected visitors. "I'm a busy man; I don't have time for—"

Monroe cut him off. "We need to talk about the murder of Ronald Waverly."

The tension in the room thickened, and Harrison's smile faded. "What do you mean?"

"It means we have evidence linking you to the crime, Vincent," Chief Monroe replied, his voice steady. "We found a bloodstained pocket watch at the festival grounds, one that belongs to you."

Harrison's eyes narrowed, and his brows knit together. "This is absurd! I had nothing to do with Ronald's death."

"We also know about your shady past," Monroe continued, pressing forward. "Your dealings in land scams and your questionable associates—these aren't just rumors, Vincent. They paint a picture of someone who would do anything to protect their reputation."

The mayor's demeanor shifted. "This is slander! You have no proof!"

Jake stepped closer, his voice firm but calm. "We have more than just the watch. We've gathered testimonies and evidence that point to you, Mayor. The truth is out."

Harrison's face paled, and I could see the gears turning in his mind, calculating his next move. "You're making a grave mistake here. I'm the mayor. This town trusts me."

"And you've betrayed that trust," Monroe said, unfazed. "You're under arrest for the murder of Ronald Waverly."

The tension escalated as Monroe placed the cuffs on Harrison, who continued to protest. "You can't do this! I'm innocent! You're making a terrible mistake!"

But as the mayor was led away, I felt a wave of relief wash over me. The community had been deceived for too long, and it was finally time to expose the truth.

As we walked out of the office, I turned to Jake, my heart still racing. "He'll never go down without a fight."

"He'll try," Jake replied, shaking his head. "But now that we have him, it's just a matter of time before everything unravels."

Back outside, the sun shone brightly, illuminating the faces of the townspeople who had gathered. Whispers circulated, and a sense of uncertainty hung in the air. But I felt a sense of hope begin to grow.

Maybe this would bring some closure—not just for Ronald Waverly but for the town that had trusted a man who didn't deserve their faith. And as I looked around at my friends, I realized we had all fought hard for this moment.

Mitz barked softly, as if sensing my feelings, and I knelt to give him a reassuring scratch behind the ears. "We did it, buddy," I whispered. "But this isn't over yet."

Jake and I exchanged glances, knowing that while we had taken a significant step forward, the battle for justice in Maple Lake was just beginning. And together, we would see it through to the end.

Chapter 21

A NEW MAYOR

The crisp autumn air hung heavily with anticipation as the town of Maple Lake buzzed with news of the mayor's arrest. I stood in the town square, flanked by Jake and Lila, taking in the scene around us. The vibrant hues of red and orange leaves painted a picturesque backdrop, a sharp contrast to the shock and disbelief etched on the faces of our neighbors.

The announcement of the mayor's arrest had spread like wildfire, and as the townspeople began to gather, murmurs of disbelief turned into passionate discussions. I could sense the underlying current of hope. Maybe now, with the truth laid bare, Maple Lake could heal from the deception that had clouded its governance.

Jake squeezed my hand, grounding me amidst the chaos. "Are you ok?" he asked, his eyes searching mine for reassurance.

"I think so," I replied, though uncertainty lingered. "It's just... so much has changed in such a short time. I never expected any of this."

"I know," he said, his voice steady. "But we'll get through it together. This is a new beginning for everyone, including us."

"So maybe now is a good time to tell you two something." Lila chimed in squeezing Max's hand.

Lila flung her hand forward to show off her sparkling diamond. "We're engaged!" She beamed.

"Oh, my goodness! Lila, Max, that's fantastic. I couldn't be happier for you guys." I eyed Lila as if to tell her I'd need all the details. "More to celebrate then."

As we moved through the crowd, I overheard snippets of conversation, most of them focused on the scandal that had unraveled. "I can't believe he was involved in all that," one woman whispered, shaking her head. "I thought we could trust him."

"Trust is hard to come by these days," another replied. "But maybe it's time for someone new to take charge."

The thought lingered in the air like the scent of baked goods wafting from the nearby festival tents. Just then, someone caught my attention—a group of townsfolk was gathered around Jake, their faces animated as they spoke. I felt a surge of pride as I listened to their words.

"You should run for mayor, Jake!" one of the shopkeepers exclaimed. "You care about this town, and we need someone with integrity at the helm."

The idea took root, and the excitement in the crowd began to build. "You would do great things for Maple Lake," another added, enthusiasm sparkling in their eyes. "We need a leader we can trust!"

I watched as Jake's expression shifted from surprise to contemplation. He hadn't just been *my* rock through this tumult; he was a pillar of the community. The more they spoke, the more it seemed like a natural fit for him.

"I appreciate your support," Jake said, raising his hands to quiet the crowd. "But I can't do this without considering what it means for my future and my family. I need to think about the responsibilities that come with this position."

The crowd murmured their understanding, but I could see the wheels turning in Jake's mind. There was something deeper at play here, and I sensed he was on the verge of making a decision that would change everything.

I beamed at Jake, sensing that this moment was important. I stepped back a bit, giving Jake the opportunity to hear the townspeople out.

As I turned away, my heart raced with anticipation for what was to come. The air was charged with a tinge of hope, and I could see the weight of Max's prior behavior had now lifted from Lila's shoulders. I was excited about what their future might hold.

I wandered back toward Jake, who was still in deep conversation with the townsfolk. I was drawn to him, the magnetic pull of his presence undeniable.

"Hey," I said softly, slipping my hand into his.

He turned to me, a smile breaking through his thoughtful expression. "That's so great about Lila and Max."

"It is. She deserves this. They are good for each other." I said, my eyes darting back to see the smiles on their faces as they chatted together like teenagers.

Jake nodded, but there was a fire in his gaze. "You know, I've been thinking a lot about what the townspeople said. About running for mayor."

I met his eyes, my pulse quickening. "And?"

"I think I want to do it," he declared, his voice firm. "This town deserves someone who will fight for them, and I believe I can make a difference. But there's one condition."

My breath caught in my throat as I felt the weight of his words. "What condition?"

Jake took a step closer, his hand tightening around mine. "I want you in my life, Molly. If I'm going to lead this town, I want you by my side as my partner. I love you, Molly Montgomery. Will you marry me?"

The world around us faded into the background as those words hung in the air, crystal clear and breathtakingly real. I felt the warmth spread through me, the happiness blooming in my heart like the autumn flowers dotting the square.

"Wow, yes, of course I will!" I exclaimed, my voice trembling with joy. "I can't believe this. It's the best festival ever!"

His smile widened as he pulled me into a warm embrace, and I felt the town's excitement bubble around us. The prospect of a double wedding began to swirl in my mind—Lila and Max alongside Jake and me, all of us standing together at the altar, promising to love and support each other through everything.

As we pulled apart, the enthusiasm of the townspeople built around us. "Did you hear that? Jake's going to run for mayor!" Someone shouted, and the crowd erupted into cheers.

Just then the loudspeaker blared, "And once again, Mr. Thompson's pumpkin has won first prize."

I couldn't help but laugh, caught up in the celebration. "This is amazing!" I said to Jake, who was beaming with pride.

The energy was contagious, and as people began to congratulate us, I felt a sense of belonging that I hadn't fully grasped until that moment. Maple Lake was my home now, and I wanted to build my life here, with Jake by my side.

"Let's find Lila and Max," I said, glancing back toward where they had been standing. "I can't wait to tell them our news!"

As we approached them, I noticed the expressions on their faces—a mix of love and excitement. Max was clearly back to his old self, and Lila was glowing.

"Jake is running for mayor... and he wants me to be his wife!" I said, grinning as I reached them.

Before I could say any more, Lila was already in my arms, her joy infectious. "I'm so happy for you both!" She exclaimed, unable to contain her excitement.

As we celebrated, the realization hit me that our lives were changing in beautiful ways. Wedding plans were already swirling in our minds, the thought of a winter double wedding sparking a flurry of ideas.

With all the love surrounding us, I could see a future bright with promise. Together, we would embrace new beginnings, challenge the shadows of the past, and create a community that thrived on trust and love.

"Let's start planning!" I said, unable to hold back my enthusiasm any longer. "Our winter weddings are going to be magical!"

"Yes!" Lila chimed in; her eyes alight with joy. "I can't wait to get started!"

As we began discussing ideas, laughter and excitement filled the air, weaving through the town square like the crisp autumn breeze.

In that moment, everything felt right, and I knew we were embarking on a journey that would forever change Maple Lake—and our lives—together.

"Oh, my goodness, there's so much to do, Lila." My mind is a blur as we walked toward the center of the festival. Mitz trotted alongside, his nose high in the air.

"Absolutely, but I'm so excited." Lila clapped.

Jake and Max followed close behind us. They eyed each other and laughed.

Made in the USA
Monee, IL
05 June 2025